PRAISE FOR THE NOVEL

"Has all the elements of a 1950s private eye yarn." *M. Ruth Myers*

"Loved this book, a classic LA Noir, with a twist of the paranormal." *M. Louisa Locke*

PRIVATE VICES

BRIGHT LIGHTS, DARK LIVES

ANDY MCKELL

Admin & Legal

Disclaimer
This book is a work of fiction. Any references to historical events, real people, or real locales are used fictitiously. Other names, characters, places, and incidents are products of the author's imagination, and any resemblance to actual events or locales or persons, living or dead, is entirely coincidental.

Cover
authorsassembler.com

ISBN
978-2-9199542-1-6

Keep Updated
andymckell.com/bibliography
Andy's Newsletter (bit.ly/andynoirs)

To my wife of over thirty years for her support and patience.

1. A THING OF BEAUTY

There's a body at my feet and a smoking gun in my hand.

I need to get this straight in my head before I share it. There's stuff I don't want to share.

I remember how it started. She came to my office—or did it begin before then?

Fog and anger and my finger pulling the trigger.

No, I have to get this straight.

Let's start with the meeting. Early September…

1951, East Los Angeles

I was in my office—up two flights, turn right, and it's at the far end. It must've been late, maybe seven, getting dark. A Wednesday. I never understood Wednesdays. Too far away from both weekends. Not that I did much at the weekend. Especially when I couldn't afford to play poker with the boys.

I was closing up. The usual things: scowling at the in-tray full of bills, checking my phone was still working, closing the inner office door, switching off the lights… Someday, I'd be able to afford a receptionist to look after these things for me.

Someday.

In the darkness, the harsh splash of neon lights from the street below splattered across the office ceiling like weapon flash or a movie theater projector.

Movietown was still making magic and bringing dreams to life with flickering lights. Spinning money out of dreams. Little changed while I was busy in Europe saving the world. Was it really five years since a Liberty ship offloaded me back onto American soil to find my mother crippled and confused by a blood clot in her brain? And the big four-oh was staring me in the face.

I didn't know how long the woman was standing in the doorway while my mind wandered. Maybe she made a sound, maybe not, but I snapped out of it and took a look.

She was a sweet shape silhouetted by the strip lighting in the hallway and topped by tumbling hair. I took in the sheath of her pencil skirt and snug, fitted jacket.

I guessed she was just asking directions for another of the petty outfits in this rat-run of a decrepit building.

I flipped on the lights. A blond beauty. Early thirties. Dark blue buttoned-up jacket. Her right hand rested on her hip while her left clutched a purse too slim to hold anything more than a handkerchief and loose change. She didn't look like a loose change kind of woman. The scarlet slash of lipstick across her strong face showed she meant business.

It was a pose. A magnificent pose. A model, actress, or something? After all, this was movietown. She was definitely *something*.

I glanced at her left hand. Bad habit of mine. Empty third finger.

"Can I help you, Miss?"

No reply. She stared at me, assessing me with those steely, gray-blue eyes in a perfect, tanned face that demanded attention.

A wide-brimmed hat would have set it off, but that would have hidden her hair.

I tried again, gesturing around the outer office. "I'm between receptionists. Come on in, Miss…?"

She took in the place with a slow, superior glance. I was embarrassed by the shabbiness surrounding her sleek perfection. Her attention rested on the bare receptionist's desk, lacking typewriter and other secretary flibbets. She took two confident steps into my domain, just as far as the desk. Staring into my eyes, she drew one elegant finger across the desk's surface, leaving a line in the dust. "And between clients, it seems." She sneered at her fingertips, rubbing them together as if scraping away something foul.

So she had the clothes, the look, and—to top it all—the attitude and the voice: a mellow delight, rich and throaty. It stirred something inside me. Clear diction, cut-glass accent. Sounded like an East Coast finishing school product.

She paused for a moment. Was she trying to decide or was it just for effect? Maybe both. She moved again, a swan on heat, prowling across the room and past me to my closed inner office door.

She didn't speak, didn't turn. She waited for me to open it for her. I took my time. It looked like she had money to spend, and I thought about those mounting bills. So I held the door for her, smiling my charming smile. I fought back the urge to hold my hand out for a tip. That would've been tasteless.

Her perfume seduced my brain as she glided past, her arm brushing my chest. Delicate, expensive, attention-grabbing.

She did that strut over to my desk and stood waiting at the visitor's chair. I didn't like her. Didn't like her attitude. She'd be a difficult client. Well, she could plant her own sweet ass on the chair without my help. I strolled around the desk and flopped into my swivel-chair. With my head cocked to one side, I looked up at her patiently while she looked down on me coldly.

I took in more details while our gazes battled it out. Immaculate grooming, fingernails painted the vicious color of her lipstick, a couple of fancy rings. Her outfit probably cost more than my car. Her car would cost more than my apartment if I could afford to buy my apartment.

My gaze won. She lowered herself slowly, elegantly, crossing her legs at the knee, making a show of it. Staring directly into my eyes to see if I was watching, she tugged down the hem of her skirt. It wasn't a demure action. It was one of those things this kind of woman did to draw attention to something in case you weren't looking. She settled down with one hand resting on the other, palms down on the bag on her lap. Relaxed, poised, posed. She looked like she owned the room.

Hell, she owned the room, the building, and half the city. A dominating woman if ever I'd stepped aside for one. And I hadn't done that in a long time. This should be an interesting conversation.

Class. Style. Self-assured. I knew the type: the type who anticipated—and got—the worship of dewy-eyed boys and older men with dark tastes or submissive secrets and private vices. Most of all, she was wealthy. I liked that last part.

Just one thing didn't fit the image. That shade of blond was as natural as the flowers in a cheap dentist's waiting room. I could almost smell the peroxide.

Otherwise, she'd taken a lot of trouble to look good. And I appreciated it.

Maybe she'd done her hair that color for some guy. But it didn't fit with her expensive tailoring and all the rest. Her outfit was a welcome, deep twilight blue at the end of a long and perfect summer's day. Her cheap hair tumbled down around slim shoulders. High heels, color-coordinated with her dress: the extra height added to her goddess-like dominance.

Was her outfit fashionable? See me shrug?

I know people, not clothes. Clothes change, people don't. Fashion is what they wear today. Tomorrow, they'll be the same people under tomorrow's fashions. But style is different. Style endures. And she had style: she oozed it. That's why the bottle-hair didn't fit. But I was patient. I knew I'd find out all about it sometime.

I really wanted to know what she needed from a cheap hack like me. That would come later, too. But for now, she wanted to tell me a story. It wouldn't be a nice story.

Most people who walked in here had some version of the same story. Usually, it's about a guy and a girl. Sometimes, there's more than two players. But they're all just different versions of the same story.

Here's hers.

2. A TALE TO TELL

I tried again. "You know my name from the sign on the door. What do I call you?"

"Lyra."

"Is that *Miss* Lyra?"

The corners of her mouth twitched like I'd said something funny, but she pursed her lips and smothered it. "Just Lyra."

"So how can I help, *Lyra*?" I always thought it sounded classier to offer help instead of paid services.

"I want you to find a man."

So far, so vanilla. Routine. I didn't have to hide any excitement. "Any particular man?"

I felt her cold stare hit me like it was all the way from Alaska.

"This one." She handed me a grainy black and white. It might have once been a four-by-four-inch photo. But the left half was missing, ripped off. The image quality was lousy. Standard room lighting, no flash. A middle-aged guy in a tux, stomach starting to spread, early balding setting in. The picture ended at the man's knees. He could be tall; he could be short. I could just make out a fancy watch and a couple of rings—one a thick wedding band, the other a pinky ring. It could have been anyone. Anyone rich.

"You have a name for him?"

She shook her head, a taut, slight headshake. I looked at the picture again. A naked, slender arm was draped over the man's shoulders. The rest of the woman was on the missing half.

"Is the woman who belongs to this arm significant?"

"No." It was a definite, final, don't-ask-again kind of no.

I looked harder. It could have been any drawing room in any big house of money. No paintings on the wall in the half I held. No lamps or vases. Dark, patterned wallpaper. Nothing to identify the room. I could've been sitting in it and I'd never have known.

"Who took the photo?"

"I do not know."

It looked a little faded, but sunlight could do that as well as time. "When was it taken?"

"I do not know."

"How did you get hold of it?"

"Someone pushed it through my letterbox."

"There's a lot you don't know."

Her expression didn't alter. She just blinked her eyes slowly, calmly. A cat considering cream.

"The cops could run fingerprints and—"

"Not the sheriff!" Again, that hard voice of command snapped out an order.

"Which sheriff? We're in the city. I meant the LAPD."

She shrugged it off. "Cops, county sheriff, same thing."

I scratched my cheek and gave a long, drawn-out, "Well..." to show how difficult this would be and how high ticket we were talking. "Let's try another tack. Tell me everything you know about him."

"He has something belonging to me." As if that explained everything.

I offered her the photo back. "Try the cops. That's the LAPD." I enjoyed making my meaning clear.

She didn't take it back. She hesitated before deciding to tell me just a little more. "I told you. No cops. I do not want to make a fuss. I simply wish to know how to contact him. To ask about what belonged to me."

I examined her face, looking for clues. First off, Lyra wasn't the type to ask for anything. She wasn't even asking me to take this job. She was giving me instructions. Most likely this "something" she wanted was letters or photos. It usually was.

"So you just want me to locate him, not to retrieve…this thing?"

"Correct."

"And no cops?"

I felt the lash of a whip in her glare. "It's not something I want some beat cop getting his dirty fingers into." A flash of emotion, maybe genuine.

"But my fingers are clean enough?" I dropped the photo on my desk and held up my hands, fingers spread, offering them for inspection.

"I heard you were…"

"Cheap?" I guessed.

"…discreet."

"From who?"

"From whom." She corrected me like a strict schoolmarm, without a pause. "And you would hardly expect me to be less discrete than I expect you to be." She leaned back in the chair.

"Miss, I don't know who you are, so discretion is a given. Okay, so I have one lousy photograph, no name, no location. Tell me about his habits, places he goes." I noticed the slight twitch in her left cheek, but I carried on as if I hadn't. "People he knows, cars he drives…"

She sat so still for so long, I thought she'd fallen asleep with her eyes open.

"I do not know what car he drives these days. I do not know his friends. Listen," she leaned forward for emphasis, "if it were so easy, I could do it myself." I felt an angry heat beneath her firmness.

She'd said "these days." Was it worth chasing that slip? Probably not. "Okay. So we have a bad photo and no information. He looks rich."

She nodded. "Very."

I tried again. "You know where this was taken?"

"No." Again, the denial was too firm, too knee-jerk.

"Okay, let's try narrow it down." I made a steeple with my fingers and leaned forward, looking serious, looking professional. "It was taken locally? I mean, this could be New York, London, Paris…"

"Locally. That is why I am looking for a *local* investigator." She spoke wearily like she was explaining the obvious to a child. Her gaze wandered over my face, maybe looking for how much she could trust me. At last, she volunteered something. "Within an hour's drive from here. That much I can tell you."

"You know how many middle-aged, rich guys live within an hour's drive from here? And how do we know this wasn't just a quick visit to the area?" I heard myself saying "we." I knew I was going to take the case. It wasn't like I had a backlog of work on the books right then. Just a backlog of bills.

She sighed, shuffling in her seat, displaying her impatience. I'd gotten the feeling she didn't like questions. "He lives around here or has a house nearby. That is all I know."

"So how do you know he lives around here?" I asked as casually as I could manage. I was pissed at this whole smoke-and-mirrors thing, this seven veils dance. Sure, I needed the work, but I also needed a client who gave me enough information to get started. I had to put her on the rack to squeeze out anything at all.

Maybe she wanted me to cuff her to the chair and beat it out of her. No, not this woman. I guessed it'd be the other way around.

She was talking again. She wasn't saying much, but at least she was talking. Slowly, quietly. "This kind of man will not travel far for his pleasures."

Interesting choice of words. "Pleasures? What kind of man is he? And how do you know?"

From her reaction, I knew I'd hit the spot. But I didn't know what that spot was. Her face held its blandness, but she spoke each word with mixed emotions trembling just below the surface. "Powerful. Domineering."

Moneyed and with that profile? It meant movietown or old money or the Mob. They were all the same in this town. And I didn't want to get mixed up with any of them. They all enjoyed their privacy too much. Too many incautious Joes walking round with missing fingers or heads. I pushed the photo back across the desk.

"I don't want this job. No starting point and a dangerous end point."

3. WEAKNESS

"I shall pay double your usual fee." With one elegant finger, she slid the image back toward me. "Whatever it is."

All she got was silence.

"And all you have to do is find where he is. I shall do the rest."

I didn't like it. I also didn't like the bills piling up with no magic fairy coming with help. Maybe Lyra was my magic fairy. Like the Blue Fairy in Pinocchio. But that made me the puppet. I threw the thought away. "Just locate him? Low-profile research? Not drawing attention to myself?"

"Or to me. Especially not to me."

My sigh signaled my defeat. But I still needed a starting point. I tried something else. "So why do you think he's local?"

"I was informed by some people I trust. I know he is in the area."

"But they didn't tell you where they saw him?"

"I could not impose upon their discretion." There she went again, hiding the information I needed to do the job.

"And you suppose this was taken locally, but you don't know where exactly?" I shoved the photo back toward her. It spun like the bottle in a Truth or Dare game. Her gaze lowered. She stared at the spinning picture like she was hypnotized.

She waited till it came to a halt then looked up without speaking.

"You know, Lyra, getting anything helpful from you, like a starting point, is like pulling teeth."

She jerked out of her reverie. Her gaze flickered back to my face again. I saw sharp points of ice in a cold, hard face.

"Okay, okay. I can ask around…Lyra. But to be honest, there's not much chance."

In fact, it wasn't a totally hopeless case. If he really was wealthy, he'd be in the society columns at charity balls, movie premieres, election candidates' fund-raising dinners…all the fancy events I didn't get invited to, but the press boys did. She seemed smart; why hadn't she thought of it herself? Or maybe she had and came up with nothing. So she should have told me and saved some cash. Or maybe money didn't matter? I still didn't understand what her game was. "What have you done yourself to find him?"

She shook her head. "I told you, I do not want to draw attention to myself. I took advice on whom to hire and was given your name. I wish to be invisible in this."

Okay, I thought, *I'll look through the press archives, the society columns. That should turn up something, but it's a lousy photo.*

"I can keep this?" My fingers reached for the torn snap. "I need it to show people, to compare with other photographs."

"Of course. But I want it back." So lady Lyra was sentimental? Unlikely. She'd need it to show others if I failed.

"Sure," I reassured her. "And did…whomever…tell you my rates?"

She opened her purse and took out an envelope. Of course, it would be cash. Cash was so deliciously anonymous. "If you are as good as I was told you are…" She pointedly glanced around the office. "This should cover expenses and a few days' work."

The flap wasn't stuck down. I lifted it and peeked inside. The top bill carried the familiar stern-faced image of Benjamin Franklin. I assumed the other three were hundreds, too. "More than enough for a few days' work." My hand moved toward the receipt book on the desk. "I'll give you a detailed breakdown and any refund at the end."

"Find him quickly and you can keep it all. And I do not want any paperwork, invoices, things like that." She fluttered her fingers in the air, dismissing such trivialities.

"Nothing more you can tell me to speed things along? I guess you need an answer fast?"

"Hardly a huge intellectual leap for someone I hope is competent. I just told you so." Brittle and ice-cold, she stood to leave, clutching her bag to her stomach.

"Yes, you did. It's about the only thing you did tell me. So how do I contact you?"

"You don't. I shall call you." Another layer of control.

I shrugged my acceptance.

"Remember, a prompt result is expected." She didn't offer a handshake. Neither did I. She just spun around on her high heels and headed for the door.

I stayed seated, enjoying the view as she swayed away. "Yes, *ma'am*."

She didn't react, just kept walking. So I enjoyed watching her prowl out of my office, listening to those heels click-clicking down the hallway to the stairs. She hadn't waited for me to play doorman this time. She knew she'd won, so she had nothing else to play for. I bet she knew I was watching her walk away.

I counted the Benjamins again; it didn't take long. One, two, three, four. A month's pay. It was way too much. The search would be over in a day or I'd come up with nothing. Her story was a pile of holes. There'd be more to tell me later, I was certain. She was leading me one step at a time. But why? I shrugged it off. I needed the cash. She'd found my weakness. But she'd known it before she walked in.

She was the type who played on a man's weaknesses. But for

what? In this case, just to make a stranger do the jumps for cash? It made no sense. I picked up the envelope and turned it over, finding nothing on the back but blank manila. It carried a hint of her expensive perfume. I ran through a few mixed emotions and shrugged.

The envelope fitted easily into my top drawer, the one whose lock still worked. Then I thought about how much was in there and slipped it instead into my inside jacket pocket. Her perfume lingered. It was a joy to the senses. That, at least, was genuine.

So her story was only half a story. But there was a girl and guy, so the beginning was fairly standard. I wondered where it would take me. But that was for tomorrow. I'd go through the motions. I'd start with the society pages going back a couple of years and see if anything turned up. If not, it was a pretty hopeless quest.

But right then, I needed to get out of that crummy office.

4. RESEARCH

I spent the next day at the library.

All the world was there, but the gossip pages and local information were all I cared about. You learn a lot about a town from the people who run it.

The first time I'd visited this library, I was greeted by some prim librarian guy in horn-rims and tweed. I couldn't take my eyes off his sweet, polka-dot yellow bow tie as he informed me I needed the sub-basement and pointed to the elevator. I caught a whiff of his cologne. Not for the weak. Then he was head-down over his magazine. I risked lung damage from the cologne, leaned over the desk, and peeped. It was an article about Judy Garland. It had a picture of her in *The Wizard of Oz*, headlined, "Friends of Dorothy." He'd seen me looking and covered it with his arm. "I said the elevators are—"

"Yeah, I heard. Over there." I'd smiled pleasantly and strolled away.

The rickety elevator was one of those birdcage items. It clanked and jerked its way down through the depths till I thought I was under the San Andreas Fault.

I always took the stairs after that when I visited the archives.

But this day was different. The archives section was as dark and gloomy as ever, with dim ceiling lights. Each reading position carried its own banker's reading lamp with a friendly, green glass shade. The guy was gone. Instead, a cute new girl sat at the desk. She raised her head as I approached and gave me a welcoming smile. The bronze nameplate on her desk read "Miss D. Grey."

Maybe she was bored. The place was, as usual, empty. In any case, I got the full attention of this pretty young librarian. Late twenties. Unflattering schoolmarm spectacles. Brunette hair modestly tied up in a bun. Cute nose.

I glanced at her left hand. Unadorned. Like I said, bad habit of mine. Maybe she noticed. I thought I detected the hint of a smile.

She *was* cute. More than cute. She could have been any pretty hopeful hitting movietown expecting to get spotted but ending up serving tables. So many bellhops and waitresses around town claiming to be "between movies."

Miss Grey wasn't that type. She'd have been talent-spotted fast. But she was hiding her talents away in the archives' gloom. She wasn't a movietown hopeful. She must have a brain. I liked that. I looked some more.

Brown eyes, partly hidden by those heavy frames; a slight upturn to her nose; high cheekbones but not too high; pointed chin but not too pointed… Yes, I liked her.

She reminded me of Donna Reed in *It's a Wonderful Life*. I'd caught the movie five years back in New York. It was Christmas 'forty-six when I got off the Liberty ship before catching the train west. I loved it. I couldn't see why it was such a flop. I still had a lingering crush on Miss Reed. I'd never had a chance to meet her, even though she lived just across town.

I guess I was smiling at my thoughts when I spoke with Miss Grey. Smiling at people does grease wheels. Or maybe she was just pleased to have some company. In any case, she gave me her whole time, suggesting new avenues to follow, bringing me folders of cuttings as well as old copies of the dailies. She even offered me tea a couple of times which must have been a rules violation.

So I drank tea and browsed through a million images of middle-aged men in tuxedos, with or without some starlet on their arms, all smiling at the public, whose hard-earned pennies had somehow ended up in their pockets.

None of them looked like our John Doe. Or maybe they all looked like him. It was hard to tell. It was a lousy photo. And all rich, middle-aged guys seemed to look the same: the same receding hairline, the same spreading waistline, the same smug grin. He was still just an anonymous guy.

To me, all these major players were anonymous unless they appeared on the front pages if I ever bothered to read them. I might recognize their names, remember vaguely what industry they owned or what scandal they'd not managed to buy their way out of. They were all in the archives record if I needed to know; mostly, I didn't care. I didn't know them, and I was happy they didn't know me.

So I eyeballed three years of pictures until they were all blurring in my mind. I leaned back and stretched my arms wide and high. My back ached. So who was this big shot who never appeared in the society pages but showed up in swell lounges? This might be the problem. If he lived a secretive life, I wouldn't find him this way.

Mob, movies, moneyed…

This was wearing me out. I was chasing a ghost.

The big station clock above Miss Grey's desk showed it was getting late. Time to go. She came over to me wearing a sweet smile as I rose. "Did you find the man you were looking for?" Nice voice. Educated but not showy like Lyra's.

I shook my head and reached for my hat.

"So you'll be back tomorrow?"

Did I detect a trace of hopefulness? "No, I think I'm done here."

Did I detect a flicker of disappointment? "But I expect I'll be back another day." I don't know why I added, "Soon."

She smiled again. It made me feel good. It was worth the effort of adding that last word.

I stood on the library steps as the streetlights flickered into life. I wished some light would flicker in this damned case. At least I'd earned my day rate. It was comforting somehow.

Some rusty-haired guy bumped into me as he hurried out the door. He mumbled something then scuttled off, face down, leaving me to gather my thoughts again. I didn't think much of it at the time.

I thought about visiting Mom. I thought about grabbing a drink. I thought about Miss Grey.

I decided not to follow up on any of those thoughts.

Instead, I dropped in on an old friend way across town. A bullet in the spine retired Harry from the FBI a few years back. These days he rolled his wheelchair around a photographic lab in his backroom for spending money and played a mean poker hand Fridays at his run-down clapboard house over toward San Bernardino. He couldn't get out much. More important, he worked miracles with light and chemicals in that back room.

There were no miracles that day.

"Sorry, pal." He pushed his spectacles high into his thinning hair and peered up at me. His pebble lenses helped for close work. Without them, he squinted hard at me just an arm's length away, perched on his worktop. This work needed good eyes. He couldn't do this for much longer. He was looking pale.

Harry always kept copies of his artistry and hung the prettiest ones on his walls. Hopeful wannabe-starlets—this damn town was full of hopefuls. The headshots and posed girlie pictures on the wall were the same as on my last visit. He wasn't getting much new work, it seemed.

He noticed me looking and chuckled. "Sure, I can't *do* anything anymore." He patted his thighs. "But I can enjoy looking.

"Anyway, can't do much with this. The negative would've been better." He shrugged. "Bad shot, bad light, bad print, grainy. Can't enhance it enough to make it worth your five bucks." He offered the photo back to me.

"How old?" I didn't take it. I wanted more.

He looked again at the image. "Depends how it's been stored. Not creased but handled often." He turned it over in his hands. "Too big for a wallet snap, not sunlight-faded like it's been on display. It's from an album or been kept in a drawer. This paper supplier went bust around Pearl Harbor time. So maybe up to ten years old."

A man could age a lot in ten years. And I'd only gone back three years in the library archives. Another seven years?

Harry was still talking, cleaning his glasses with a spotless handkerchief, breathing on the lenses, polishing them, holding them up to the light to inspect for smudges, then repeating the process. "So you looking for this guy, huh? Anything to do with the Mansion is usually dirty. Surprised at you. Things getting tough, yeah?"

I didn't pick up on what he'd just said. My focus was on seven years of society pages, maybe more. I was picturing more hot tea and warm smiles from Miss Grey. "Hmm? Tough? Yeah, things are always tough. So much for the post-war boom, eh? It don't seem to reach down as far as me."

"Nor me." He hung the glasses back on his face and focused on me. "So you want me to fake a shot with a client's wife on the end of the arm? Or I can add some random floozy if you want." He gestured at the display on the wall. I noted the crucifix he said his mother had given him, nestling between a pretty swimsuit blonde and a nude redhead. "Take your choice. I know a lot of girls who need the cash."

"I don't do that kind of work, Harry. And I never will."

He shrugged. "I know. I was only joking." He grinned then turned serious. "Just remember me if and when."

I nodded. I never would, and he knew it. But it looked like he needed the work. He was a friend, even though he emptied my wallet every time he sat in on our low-stakes poker games. "The medical bills are crippling," he always joked, as if to apologize.

"Can you run me off a couple of copies?"

"Won't take long. I'll dry 'em overnight and mail 'em to you."

I tapped out a Lucky and offered him one.

He looked like I'd asked his mother for a date. "Christ! Not here, pal." He indicated the chemicals and paper stored neatly around the room. "Porch or card room."

So we sat smoking on his front porch, shooting the breeze in the warm evening air, talking about nothing in particular. Then I left him to do whatever he did after hours.

5. JIMMY'S BAR

Next day, I was in the archives again, looking back ten years. Miss Grey seemed pleased to see me.

More smug, grinning faces. More starlets, fancy dinners, movie premieres…

And there was more tea. I might even get to like tea.

The evening was creeping in by the time I slid into the car. Again, Miss Grey seemed disappointed to see me leave. Again, my eyes ached from scanning so much printed saccharin. Again, I'd found nothing.

I sat in the car, thinking about nothing for a minute or two, then just started driving aimlessly. It was Friday night, I realized.

I didn't want to go home. Too empty.

I didn't want to go to a city bar. Too crowded.

I didn't feel like losing money I didn't have to Harry and the boys. Too expensive.

Without a plan, I cruised west along Venice Boulevard and turned into Lincoln, heading for Santa Monica. It was a fine, warm evening. I kept wanting to put down the top, but I'd had to trade in the used convertible for something even older, more used, and more affordable.

I was tired and jaded and not making the office rent. I felt like

I'd seen it all. Yeah, I'd seen too much; that was for certain. I didn't know what I was looking for anymore. Time to find a new bar, new faces, new…new something.

Maybe someone like Miss Grey was what I needed. Only time would tell. I felt a little better as I thought about it. Just a little.

It wasn't just Lyra's fake hair, fake story, fake sincerity. It was my life, I guess. I needed a change.

I slowed down at Santa Monica Pier. The ocean sparkled in the distance. Decision time. South to Venice Beach or north along the Pacific coast? And where to after that? I was still weighing up the options when I found I'd already turned north.

The palm trees swayed high above me as I drove. Hell, I loved those trees. I cruised along the coast road, not paying much attention, till I ran out of street lights. I thought about turning around. There was nothing between here and Bayville. I didn't want to see Bayville again. Ever.

I found a turning on the ocean side. A dirt road, curving back to the south and heading down out of sight toward the water. I spun into it to make my turn back to the city. My headlights picked out a sign near the top of the slope. Peeling paint words on a rotting wooden board invisible from the road. I squinted to make out the words. "Jimmy's Bar." Plain and simple.

Plain and simple was just what I needed. Under the words, a faded red arrow pointed down the slope. Could it still be in business? Hard to find, hidden away…private, maybe. Most likely closed down long ago. Well, I had nothing else to do, and my job was chasing up lost things, lost people, lost lives. I'd give it a few minutes of my valuable Friday evening time. I headed down toward sea level.

On the right lay the endless Pacific, peaceful as a prowling shark, dark as spilled blood. A long, shimmering stripe reflecting the low-hanging moon dappled from the horizon to the rocks below. Pretty. To my left, the cliff-side loomed up to the highway, though I couldn't see any car headlamps on the road above. Yeah, this was pretty private.

The road wound down till I was almost at the ocean but with no hint of a bar. I was ready to give up, already looking for a place to turn around.

And there it was.

Jimmy's Bar.

It was an oversized, single-story cabin with a parking lot on the land side that could hold twenty but was empty right now. Lights shone dimly through curtained windows. It looked run-down like the sign, but it seemed to be in business, and by then, I really needed a drink. I pulled into the vacant spot of my choice and strolled over. The ocean made its presence felt. The salt air hit me first then the gentle crash of breakers beyond the cabin. The door had those fiddly fake curtains, tied back in the middle. Yellow shellfish on a faded red background. Classy. I peered inside. It was empty except for a barman, polishing glasses. Why did they do that with unused glasses? Filled the time, I guessed. Obsessive barkeeps. Or part of the training. Who cared?

I strolled in, and he looked up, unsurprised, as if I wasn't the only guy in the place. "Good evening, sir. What can I get you?" Neat, slicked-back, black hair and an oriental tilt to the eyes, white jacket like some upmarket steward. Warm smile that reached his eyes, so maybe it was genuine. I perched on a bar stool and named my brand.

"You Jimmy?" I asked as he set up the drink.

"Yes. But this place was Jimmy's Bar for long, long time." He spoke without looking up from the pouring, hints of the Far East in his accent.

I just nodded. The place looked neat, with old-fashioned décor. A few bar stools stood tall and empty along the counter. The half-dozen alcoves along the wall had paneled dividers for privacy or maybe for intimacy. Their seats were beige. I never liked beige. A faint damp odor hung about the place, maybe from the ocean. No trace of stale tobacco smoke.

The walls were hung with Indian relics I assumed were fake. This didn't look like a genuine antiques kind of place. Some rugs, a couple of spears, a couple of feathered headdresses straight out of a John Wayne movie and other knick-knacks.

The Indian decorations were all out of place with an oriental barman, or maybe he was out of place with them. It all added to the strangeness of the place. Maybe that was its appeal. It didn't appeal to me.

"So, Jimmy, when do you get busy?"

He looked up. "All the time." He grinned a little like he'd just made a joke.

I didn't get the joke.

"You live at the back of the shop?" I really didn't care but talking filled the silence.

"Why do you ask?" He seemed genuinely interested in knowing why.

"No cars out front."

"Ah, *that* is why you asked. I see." He turned away to place a few polished tumblers on a shelf.

I lost interest. I looked around. I should finish my drink and get back to the living world.

There were two doors other than the entrance. The one at the end of the bar carried restroom symbols. The other was set in what I guessed was the back wall. A wooden ring maybe a foot across and draped with feathers hung above the rear door.

I made one, final attempt at being sociable. It never came easy at the best of times, and this was not the best of times. "You got a garden?" I nodded at the back door. I didn't bother hiding my mockery.

His eyes twinkled. "Better than garden. Much better. Why not take stroll outside and find out?"

I didn't budge. "Gimme a hint, so I know it's worth my time."

"Ocean view from the old days. You can get back lost time, just sitting and thinking."

It sounded crazy. It was probably his loneliness. Was this even a licensed bar? Jimmy wasn't urging me, wasn't interested in knowing if I'd go, wasn't curious about how unimpressed I'd be when I came back in. He just stood there, calm, patient, polishing. He broke the silence with some philosophy. "You know what they say? *In vino veritas.*"

"In wine there is truth?" I shrugged. It was a good enough marketing slogan for a bar. I found it worked with whisky, too. "Okay, I'll play along. I'll take a fresh Scotch with me."

I looked down and found he'd already topped me up. He knew I'd go for it. Or the drink was to keep me there longer. The whole thing was probably a delaying tactic. You go to a bar: it's empty, you drink up and leave, another guy walks in and sees an empty bar… People stay if they see others around. Most likely, Jimmy just wanted to keep me there longer until someone else arrived. But that event was unlikely.

Ocean view? Sounded good. I was always attracted to the ocean. Way back, Mom and me'd headed west till the Pacific blocked the way.

So why not? I grasped the tumbler and strolled toward the door to "Jimmy's Special Place."

He called after me. "The old Yurok Indian tribal name for this bay means 'Catcher of Fog Dreams.' Legend says a man can find what he is looking for when the fog rolls in."

I didn't know peyote cactus grew this far north. It sounded like those Yurok medicine men had help from a special medicine. But even without peyote mescalin, those old shamans knew their tricks, how to sell a fantasy. They were great dreamweavers long before movietown appeared.

"No fog tonight," I countered.

"Not yet." He smiled a secretive, knowing smile. He was being deliberately mysterious and enticing. A good salesman. But what was I buying? Maybe he really was a shaman? A Chinese shaman?

What did I have to lose but a few otherwise uncommitted Friday night minutes?

So I bought the dream and stepped through the doorway.

I hadn't realized how much the wide bay curved at this point. From here, I couldn't see the twinkling of city lights along the coastline in either direction. Across to my right was a huge pile of rocks supporting a sleeping lighthouse. No light. Dead, not sleeping. To my left, a high, crumbling cliff face that looked ready to tumble into the Pacific if anyone breathed too hard. I was standing on a wooden platform, a boardwalk, clinging to the low rocks at the back of the cabin. A handrail ran the length of the building, broken only by a gap giving access to a twenty-foot walkway overhanging the waters. A wooden chair and a small, round table graced the far end. There was no handrail protecting a drunk from staggering over the side into the water. But there were no drunks. Just me, miserable with my own sense of…whatever it was.

Between the lighthouse and the crumbling cliffs stretched the vast expanse of ocean that generations of settlers had struggled and died to reach. Black waters dappled by the distorted, phantom moonlight. The stars sparkled high above in the darkest of skies without a trace of city lights' glow. Maybe I could get back lost time, like Jimmy said. It was truly beautiful. And it was all mine tonight. Mine alone.

Okay, I'd bought the line. Here I was. I might as well enjoy it. I shrugged and ambled toward the chair. The table was the right height and in the right position for my Luckies pack and tumbler. Jimmy, or someone, knew how to make a man welcome. I eased down and took in the view.

I listened to the quiet waves that had struggled all the way from Japan, only to peter out, exhausted, six feet below my scuffed black shoes. Was it worth their effort? It was relaxing. It was lulling. I listened to the swoosh, swoosh of the waves and closed my eyes. My mind wandered over Lyra's story, over Lyra herself, whoever she really was…

Maybe I dozed off; maybe I just chased dreams. I didn't know how long I was there.

I glanced at my watch. It told me I'd been here no time at all, just a few minutes. I looked around.

The fog Jimmy predicted had rolled in from nowhere in those brief moments. I didn't see it gathering. Did I hear a foghorn's distressed cow moan from somewhere? Far away or nearby? From somewhere, a radio softly played 'Moonlight Serenade.' Jimmy hadn't had the radio on, and there were no buildings nearby. Could've been a car radio. Lucky Jimmy: another customer got lost down here.

Maybe I heard a soft footstep or a floorboard creak or a deep breath. There was someone behind me.

I came fully alert, my back straightening, my body tensed to turn. I listened for the click of a safety catch.

My hand slipped inside my jacket as a reflex. Was it Jimmy? Or was it someone wanting the chair?

I smelled the perfume before I could yank my head around to look. It was familiar, but I couldn't place it.

Who was this woman? I needed to see her. I began to turn.

A touch on my shoulder made me freeze. Damn! How'd she get so close without me noticing?

"Please don't turn around." A request, not a warning. Gentle. Female. Twenties, maybe early thirties. Calm. Unthreatening. It sounded like a California accent.

"Okay." But I kept my hand on my automatic, just in case. "Nice view."

"The fog hides the ocean, so there is no view, if that was some ironic comment." I could hear her amusement. It sounded like she spoke through a smile.

I found myself looking out toward the hidden waters. Did I see the hint of an occasional fuzzy glimmer of light over to the right as if the lighthouse had come alive? I guessed it only lit up in the fog.

I forced my muscles to relax, to appear calm. "I like to know who's behind me. You have a name?"

"Verity."

I knew a Verity once. Long ago and far away. But she was just a kid I used to know in Bayville. "Okay, I'll call you Verity. So what brings you out here?" For an opening line, it was pathetic, but mostly it was safe.

"You."

I rolled it around in my head for a while. "Sounds good. Go on, build up my ego a little more. I enjoy it." Did Jimmy have a stock of hookers hidden away somewhere nearby? I remembered not hearing a car arrive.

"You need something. And it's not a hooker."

Was she reading my thoughts? "Agreed. So run along, sister, and leave me to my dream chasing."

"You need to know who the woman Lyra is and what her true story is."

What? She knew about Lyra? A setup? This "Verity" must've followed me here. This could be no coincidence, not in this lost place. But there'd been no car engine.

Okay, I was playing Lyra's game and playing Jimmy's game, so I'd play this one too. "And you have the answers? What will it cost me?"

She paused for so long, I began to think she'd tiptoed away. I waited, holding still, face to the fog and hand in my jacket.

"You'll only find out when it's too late." A trace of sadness. It wasn't a threat.

I'd had enough. I stood up fast and spun around, drawing my automatic.

In the twenty feet between me and the bar door were only a few stray wisps of fog.

6. NOT A HOOKER

I holstered the gun as I raced to the door and burst through.

"A good dream, sir?" The place was still empty except for Jimmy behind the bar. Calm. Grinning. Knowing.

Was she in the restroom? I'd see her when she came out if I waited. There was something I could check. Ignoring Jimmy's calm gaze, I hurried out the main door. The fog had cleared. The parking lot was empty except for my car.

I stormed back to the counter and banged my fist on it, so hard it hurt. "Where did she go?" I expected a shrug, a show of innocence, a claim of ignorance, even a hit for cash.

"Where she always goes." Jimmy tapped the side of his head, that irritating, calm smile fixed to his face. "It's just your dream, sir. Just your dream."

I stared at him, confused and angry. He was not intimidated. He just kept on doing barkeep make-work. He must have had the shiniest tumblers in the state.

My hand hurt. I was tired. The girl had gone—if she'd really been there. Somehow, it didn't seem worth the effort. I threw down a few coins and headed for the door again.

"Until next time!" Jimmy's voice was cheerful and confident.

Tough luck for him. I wasn't coming back.

———

Sunday, I dropped in on Mom at the retirement home.

A pretty swish place, so much better than a bleak state institution. A big house in a quiet area with its own grounds. I couldn't have paid the fees. Someone anonymous had set up a trust fund while I was away in Europe. The manager wouldn't tell me who it was. The doctors wouldn't tell me. The bank wouldn't tell me. The manager said I'd need a court order, but the fund would be terminated if the donor was identified. I was over a barrel. In the five years since I got back from the war, I'd gotten used to it. She was being cared for in a way I couldn't provide. So I'd shrugged and accepted it.

I found Mom in the lounge with a few of the other "girls." The nurses called them girls. Like Mom, they were mostly in their sixties. She looked drained, pale, and tired. Tired of living, maybe.

Mom smiled her warm, sweet smile when I said hello and bent to kiss her cheek. She even lifted her face a little to meet the kiss when she realized what I was doing. That cheered me. She was clearer than she'd been for a while. I think she knew who I was this time. Maybe.

It didn't last. I talked about the usual things: when I was a kid, moving to LA, vacations, the quiet Thanksgivings and Christmases, distant relatives long-dead but still alive to her, scrapes I'd gotten into… I didn't talk about Dad. I didn't remember much about him. He never got back from the First War, and I nearly lost it in the second one.

Her lips curved into a tight smile, and she nodded, pretending to remember, like she always did. But she grew tired. "I'll be letting you go now." It was her polite way of telling me to leave her alone. "But," she said, looking around, confused, "where is she?"

"Who, Mom?" I had no idea who she meant.

"You know." Her eyes took on a wicked glow as if she were

nudging me in the ribs. "Your lady friend. Oh, I know her name, what is it? Can't think right now."

It was no use explaining I'd come alone. "She's just left, Mom. She had to go. I'll bring her with me next time." I hated having to tell lies, but the truth got too complicated for her, and she would fret.

"It's her perfume. I can smell her perfume."

"Yes, Mom. It's hers." It must have been Lyra's scent on the envelope in my pocket. I gathered up my hat and stood to leave.

"A bit expensive for you, my boy. But she's worth it." She winked at me.

"Yes, she is." I bent to kiss her, but this time she didn't respond. She was concentrating, digging for an elusive thought. "Mom, I'll see you next week." She would forget I'd been there the minute I was out of her sight.

"I know that perfume…" She spoke like she was dragging the memory from wherever it lay hidden in the fog. Then her face lit up in a wicked grin again. "Ahh…!" She beckoned me to come closer. I leaned in. She whispered, "You lucky boy! Let her know I haven't told anyone. Not her dad. No one. Tell her." She chuckled a dirty chuckle in my ear then closed her eyes and rested her head on the chair back. It was a familiar position she liked to doze in.

I sat again and watched her for a while as she slipped into sleep. And all the while, I thought about the past, when she was whole. I kissed her cheek again and tiptoed away.

———

Next day, I got a call from Maria.

Sounded like she needed company. I wasn't in the mood. But there was an edge to her voice. She sounded more than just lonely. Hell, why would Maria ever be lonely?

She was a dancer. "I'm not a hooker," she always insisted,

those dark eyes flashing a warning and a hidden blade always in easy reach.

Maria was fun to be with if you like a beautiful, tough-as-nails conniving woman with a soft, caramel center, bursting with passion in every breath she took. She had reasons enough to hate men, from when she was a pretty teenager and got outnumbered one day on the way home. It took a long time to earn her trust and work your way down to that soft center. Easier to get to the Earth's core. We'd met when she'd taken the wrong guy into some dark alleyway and it had gotten out of hand.

Yeah, it's an old story. She seemed cursed.

I first met her in a hookers' alleyway a few years back, soon after I got back home and set up shop with a shiny new PI license but no office.

I'd been tailing some cheating husband one night in east LA. The wife was paying me well with hubby's money. But I lost him in the red-light district. My day was over. I was thinking about a warm, soft bed when I heard a woman's screams from the alley across the street.

The few folks on the sidewalks all went real deaf when those screams sounded. But not me. I'd always been a sucker for a damsel in distress. It's part of my charm. It's part of my curse.

I turned into the deeper darkness where the neon and street-lights didn't reach and saw two shadows grappling.

It was obvious which was the woman: the slimmer, shorter shadow-within-shadows, the one pressed against the wall by a larger-looming lump. He was beating the life out of her, raging, yelling foulness. I hated that.

"Not my face! Please, not my face."

I'd heard enough. Another of my anger bouts hit me.

He never heard me coming. It was easy. I grabbed the back of his collar, jerked him backward fast, and kicked the back of his right knee as hard as I could. He yelped and swayed toward me, losing balance, letting go of the girl's throat, arms windmilling to regain his balance. I pulled harder on his collar, and he was tumbling down, fat ass over great gut. I punched him hard as he fell, just the once. Then I introduced the tip of my shoes to his gut a few times, just to make sure he'd gotten the message and would stay down. He stayed down.

I turned to his victim, expecting gratitude. But she was still on a combat high. "Madre de Dios, you almost lost me his wallet!" That was an angry, fiery Latina voice if ever I heard one. She stooped and collected her bag from the filth in the alleyway.

"Damn it, girl. You a pain hooker?"

"I am not hooker!" It was a snarl. Her hand flicked in and out of her bag. I heard a snick. Stray moonlight glinted on the blade she held pointed at me. "I am dancer."

"Okay, okay." I raised my hands in front of me, palms facing her. I took a step back, speaking gently, trying to calm her down. "Dancer. You're a dancer."

She scowled at me. "Good." She hesitated. "I guess I owe you something." She didn't sound convinced. It sounded more like a shrug. "I buy you drink, c'mon." She made the blade vanish and slung the bag over her shoulder. I realized I'd been holding my breath. I exhaled slowly.

The stench of this tunnel between the anonymous and uncaring buildings hit me as I breathed in again. Urine and rotting garbage and stale beer. It was where that bastard belonged. I didn't. I wanted to be somewhere else, anywhere else. Her offer sounded good.

The girl paused only to add her own shoe's toe-mark to the guy's belly. He didn't make a sound. I heard the clickety-click of heels along the alleyway and followed. What else could a man do?

As she reached the street, the lights caught her face, and I caught my breath. For a second, I thought I saw Private Rico's sweet little sister the day I told her how he'd fallen bravely and honorably and hadn't suffered.

What was a girl like her doing in a—

Okay, stupid question. She was maybe twenty. She was a

beauty. Apart from the red marks on her face that'd turn purple later and the blood trickling from her lip.

Sweet, caramel-tanned skin and long, straight black hair tumbling in a mess over her face and shoulder. Dangling useless from the tangled hair was a scarlet bow that almost matched her skin-tight dress.

That dress was too damn short. And it was so tight I could see it was the only thing she wore. And she filled it with curves. Too much makeup. Jaded eyes that had seen more than they ever wanted to see. True hooker styling. But somehow, she made it look stunning.

She led me to a bar across the street. Casa de Los Angeles. Inventive.

Through the smoke haze, I made out a bar-girls-and-booze saloon that fit well in that district. A couple of the girls on the plush red seating nodded to her. None took their main attention from whichever customer they were wrapped around. None seemed to notice her disarray. Maybe my presence kept them away. Maybe they'd cluster around her, clucking and hugging, after I left. I hoped they would.

The customers seemed to know her. A couple of guys called out greetings, "Hey, Maria, come sit here," one patting the empty seat next to him, another patting his knee. "Have a drink, then maybe *un poco de diversión*?" They ignored me. She ignored them. They ignored me with indifference. She ignored them with contempt.

So she was called Maria.

She propped her elbows on the counter, leaning so low her cheap wooden crucifix swung loose, advertising her cleavage. Her rear thrust out toward the drinkers. More advertising.

Maria—or her low-cut dress—caught the barkeep's eye.

"Two doubles, Joe. And booth seven, after." Her young voice carried authority. The thuggish barman nodded. I doubted his name was Joe. All barkeeps in the red-light district are called Joe. I blame the movies.

Maria primped her hair a little then pulled out a man's wallet from somewhere. She started rifling through it but caught my look and glared back, challengingly. "I was lifting it from him when you sailed in. If he'd run, I'd get *nada* for my pains." The man she called Joe served up the tumblers and turned away.

Her eyes gave me a calculating up-and-down. She spoke quietly as if to herself. "Not bad. Not bad for an old man. Forty-five, maybe? Married, I guess, with a house on a quiet street, two kiddies, and a leetle puppy? Working late hours screwing some sweet and boring secretary who's busy tonight so you come here looking for a taste of sweet Mexican *chica*?"

Yeah, I'd had a bad war, but I wasn't a washed-up mid-forties. Not for another few years. The rest of her insults passed me by.

I grabbed the drink. "All wrong." I took a gulp. It was cheap rotgut, probably straight from Joe's bathtub.

She smiled, knowingly, without a trace of warmth. "So let's say I believe you. You expect thanks, in any case. Come into my office." She walked away, aiming herself at the quiet booths at the back of the bar.

Maria moved with the natural, sensuous sway of a cat. Sure, I was watching her ass.

It took her a moment to realize I hadn't followed. She turned back, a puzzled look on those delicious, dark features. I took another slug of whatever it was pretending to be Scotch and waited, considering her. She cocked her head to one side, such a cute gesture, and waited, too. It was a Mexican standoff.

Slowly, a smile grew on her lips. She raised a hand to push her hair back behind her ear, revealing the soft line of her neck. She raised her tumbler and slid it along the soft flesh of exposed throat, leaving a trail of condensation. "Jus' a leetle dreenk, *señor*?"

She could be whatever she thought the guy with the cash wanted her to be. I guessed she was trying to find out what I wanted her to be. She was play-acting some simple whore from across the border. I hated it. I pushed my tumbler away and turned to go.

"Hey, why the dark face, mister Sir Lancelot?" She seemed surprised.

I ignored her. We had an audience of mocking male faces full of hopes that I'd vanish soon and leave her available. I ignored them, too. I grasped the door handle.

"Hey, meester, you wan' your billfold back?"

Billfold? That stopped me. I checked. Empty back pocket. She was good, real good. I never felt a thing, never knew she was ever close enough. She must have lifted it while we were standing over her attacker.

She dangled my wallet between finger and thumb at the end of her outstretched arm like some kind of bait. Smiling like a woman totally in control, she headed for her private booth.

I shrugged at the audience, smiled weakly, and followed her. What else could I do?

The booth lay at the far end of the long room, its partition shielding us from the rest of the bar. Very private. Very dim. Very red. Red plastic seat covering and red velvet wallpaper. Maria sat and slowly, deliberately, crossed her legs so her dress rode high, watching my reaction. She rifled through my billfold, breaking off only to pat the seat next to her and smile her professional smile.

I sat heavily on the bench across the table from her and held out my hand for the wallet. "I know how much was in there."

Her smile didn't flicker. She reached out to stroke my hand. "So what's your name, my hero?"

I pulled my hand away. "You know my name. You read my ID. And I'm not interested."

She scowled. "You not staying? Okay, I gotta go, mister Sir Lancelot. I got makeup to redo. Cover the red marks. Then a driver's license to sell and maybe a wife to tell. Then back to work. A girl got bills to pay."

I grabbed her arm as she started to rise. "I can get you work. Proper work. Modeling or something."

She glared down at my restraining hand then back to my face. "Sure. You know a man. An' all I gotta do is…?" Harsh, cynical, mocking. But she sat again.

"Not like that. I mean for real."

"Listen, mister, I don't need no pimp, and I know how to get a modeling job in this city." She spat out the words. But she stayed seated. "And I don't need no john getting sweet on me." Her voice had softened. She sounded warmer and perhaps a little coy. Playing another part?

"I'm not a john."

"You mean you won't pay for it." That snarl was back. "And you a private investigator. Ex-cop, I bet, friends in Vice, gonna turn my screws?"

"Lady, you sure go through a man's paperwork fast."

"Yeah. Comes with the job. But I see no photos of wifey or leetle kiddies. No girlyfriend pictures." She was gloating. Then her voice changed. She sounded like a cop pouncing on some guy he knew was guilty. "So who's the old lady photo? You like old ladies? Or is this your mommy?"

I snatched it back, checked the contents. The important stuff was all there. "Forget it." The bitch knew how to hit way below the belt. I stood and stalked out, ignoring the catcalls from the drunks.

I drove home and got myself drunk. On my own.

7. INVITATION

There are some things you just can't shake off. Like a liquor habit, like nose candy, like gum on your shoe.

A few weeks after I met Maria, my office phone rang. It was a rare event, so I enjoyed the sound for a while before picking up. At least I knew it was still working.

"Hello, Sir Lancelot." Mexican accent.

"Yeah?" I heard my own irritation.

"You do remember little lost Maria?" I could almost hear her pouting. "I got your number off your card."

I hadn't counted the business cards when I checked my wallet. They were just cheap pasteboard. "Do I want to hear from you?" I wasn't being pleasant. Our first conversation still stung. I'd thought—I'd hoped—it would be our last.

"Aww…I wanted to be sorry. Can I be sorry?" I pictured her, sad eyed, almost pleading.

"Business slow?"

"You cruel man. I just wanted to be sorry. Let me buy you another drink and you choose what we talk about."

I thought it over.

"Listen, I got me a job. A real job. Like you say. Uniform and all." She giggled. "Wanted to let you know. To celebrate. Wanna come to my place and see my uniform?"

Uniform? Car wash, waitress, maid, who knew? Was it just another role she was playing? Dressing up for the sugar daddy, even though I had no sugar? I hated her right then. There was no way I was taking the bait...

"Okay." Hooked, defeated. "Where?"

She gave me her address. East Los Angeles, of course. The Hispanic district. It wasn't far.

I went.

Gum on my shoe.

It wasn't a uniform. It was a nightclub's cigarette girl outfit. Black, trimmed with white, it was a tight, halter-neck bodice and a skater's short skirt puffed up with those frilly, flouncing, petti-coat things. The vision was finished off by stilettos and silk stockings held up by black garters.

"Don't I look good?" She turned this way and that, hands on her hips, showing it off. She looked damn good.

"Yeah. You look like a cheap tart."

"Noooo...I used to be cheap. Not anymore." She seemed delighted at the price hike, totally missing my point.

"Take it off."

"Now? Oh, you bad man."

"No. I mean change into something decent."

She looked downcast, then her face lit up again. "Ah! You gonna take me somewhere nice? Now I understand." She twirled on the spot and wobbled off on those ridiculous heels into another room. I assumed it was her bedroom. I didn't check. Instead, I looked around her tiny living room. Basic furniture, frilly pillows, and curtains.

There was a photo of a young girl and an older woman, too old to be Maria's mother. Behind them was some small town store, wooden, weathered, old. The sign over the door read "Mercado Delgado" and gave the address and phone number. The photo stood in an expensive frame, maybe the priciest item in the room. Otherwise just a few cheap trinkets and a crucifix on the wall.

"You didn't ask where I was working," she called out through the door she had left open. I stood to one side so I couldn't see through. "It's called the Mansion."

Now I knew, and it was worse than I'd feared. I knew about the Mansion. It was an illegal casino fronting for something even darker, something even more illegal, where the untouchable rich enjoyed their private vices. A Mob business. It took me a while to reply.

"I know it. From when Joey Milan ran it after the war."

"Mr. Caldera runs it now."

I'd heard they'd brought in some guy from Reno to replace Joey. But the Mob's the same, no matter the name and the face.

"Which part of the Mansion?" I really didn't want to hear the answer.

"What do you mean? It's a casino. I serve small drinks and get big tips." She was laughing.

I was relieved. I guess someone had to work front-of-house. It could have been worse. Much worse.

———

Then she just slipped in and out of my life for a while. Gum on my shoe. And she never touched my money again.

So there I was, the week after I'd met Lyra, and Maria was calling me.

"Just wanna talk." So Maria wanted my ears this time. A guy had to accept whatever crumbs she threw down unless he was rich enough to call the shots.

It was a Monday, not my busiest day at the office. "Sure, I'll be free in an hour or two."

"Oh…meester big detective, you make a girl wait so long for her big, strong knight in the shining armors?" She always turned on the pleading, big-eyed, simple whore when it suited her.

Sometimes, I wasn't sure who she really was. I didn't think even she knew for sure.

Anyway, it was pointless. She knew it didn't work on me. I wasn't going to take the bait.

"Okay. Your place?" Like I said, it didn't work on me. Not at all. But when she clicked her fingers, I came running, every time. Why not? She served up a mean breakfast.

"No. I'm at Hollywood Roosevelt. See you down in the foyer in a half hour, after I get dressed. Drinks are on me." So Maria had overnighted at a swish hotel. She was coming up in the world. Or maybe going down in it.

I agreed and hung up. Right away, I got another call. From another woman. It never rained, but it sure did pour.

"Good morning. This is Lyra." Of course it was. No one else I knew spoke like that.

"I was just wondering what progress you had managed to make as yet." Cold, distant, formal. A million miles away from Maria's fire. Even the way Maria walked screamed out an unconscious, natural passion. Not at all like Lyra's deliberate strut. I tried not to think about Maria.

Lyra was a fake. As fake as Maria pretended to be. But Maria was real. Whatever she was pretending to be at any moment and whoever she appeared to be, she was always Maria underneath. All the parts she played were just aspects of herself. I'd heard it's called acting.

I forced my thoughts back to Lyra. "I got nothing yet. You didn't give me much to go on, and it's only been a couple of days."

"Would a bigger advance make things go quicker? Or a different incentive? Perhaps if I were to drive over to your apartment and discuss it…?" She let it hang.

"Gimme a few more days. I'm waiting to hear back from a few people." I knew it was baloney, but she was paying me for something. I hadn't found out what yet, and I had to go through the motions.

"Oh." She sounded disappointed. At my lack of progress or at turning down her offer, I couldn't tell. "Very well. I shall call again." It sounded like a threat. She hung up.

I locked up the office and left for my appointment with Maria. It wasn't like there was a queue in my reception.

————

Maria was waiting at a corner table, back from the main body of the plush foyer, where she could survey the area and be seen by everyone. Over-sized dark glasses hid her eyes. The rest of her face looked tired. She'd been working late, working hard. But she still looked stunning.

Like I said, she'd come up in the world, or maybe down. A rich john was still a john in my book. And that same book said a guy who paid to beat up women was just a rich thug. She'd drifted in and out of my life like a tax man. But at least she always bought the drinks; the tax man never did.

I heard nothing for months, then suddenly, she wanted something.

Maria skipped the formalities. "Come to the Mansion Saturday."

"That's a joke?"

She shook her head. I couldn't make out her eyes behind those big dark lenses.

"Not a good idea. And I'm doing fine, thanks for asking."

"Is a good idea. You must come. Someone wants to see you. You got a tux?"

"It's at the cleaners."

She scowled. "Yeah, your imaginary receptionist took your imaginary tux to be cleaned. You cheap man, you don't have one. I know it already." Maria opened her bag and drew out a manila envelope. She slipped it across the table with her fingertips.

"Get a tux. A good one. Look like a success, not like a doorman."

Her blood-red fingernails reminded me of Lyra's. Another beautiful woman slipping me another envelope. Things were starting to repeat themselves. "What's this?"

"You'll see. We got a girl gone missing. Someone wants to see you."

"Someone can come to my office." I pushed the envelope back toward her. This envelope-sliding routine was getting too familiar.

"No." She shook her head, resting two fingers on the manila and pushing it back to me again. "You have to come. To understand."

I thought about it. Another half-story, another envelope. I changed the subject. "Maybe you can help me with something. I'm looking for a man—"

"Oh, you never told me!" Her lips pursed.

"I mean professionally." That didn't sound any better. "For an investigation." I showed her the photo of Lyra's missing man.

A cursory glance and a shrug said it all.

"Look again. He'd be older now, maybe ten years older?"

"What are you saying?" I'd never seen her truly shocked. I wasn't seeing it now. "Ten years ago, I was a little girl!"

My sigh spoke for me. I tried again, one step at a time. "This is the only photo I have of him. It's old. He'll have changed." I felt myself growing old on this case.

"So come to the Mansion and check for him there."

"At the Mansion?"

"Yeah, same wallpaper."

Now I remembered Harry had said the photo was likely taken there. Damn it. I'd been thinking about the library and Donna instead of listening.

Maybe I *should* check out the Mansion.

"How about a woman—"

"Now you want a woman? Is leetle Maria not enough for you?" She stroked my forearm and pouted.

I ignored her. "She's about so tall in heels." I indicated with my hand. "Blue eyes, bottle-blond, well-spoken. Hard-bitten."

"I know lotsa blondes, all from bottles." She'd lost interest. "Should I go blond, you think?" She twisted a strand of her jet-black hair between her fingers and examined it. She was back in her own world.

"No, I don't. She's well-dressed, a man-eater…"

Another shrug. "Got a name?"

"Told me it was Lyra."

Maria shook her head. "No bells ringing. But so high, baby blues and a peroxide wash could be anyone in this town." Her gaze wandered across the guys in the foyer. She had other priorities.

I nodded. It was a long shot but just might have paid off. I never turn down a good coincidence.

She looked bored. "Have to go. Some of us gotta work."

Maria called back over her shoulder as she swayed toward the street door, every male eye in the place on that attention-grabbing motion. "And get a haircut!"

One of the guys watching her glanced over at me. I knew him from somewhere, but I couldn't place him. Ginger hair and loud tie. Maybe he was the guy outside the library? Coincidence? He folded his newspaper and headed for the street door.

I forgot about him and looked down at the envelope.

The Mansion? I wondered what Maria had gotten into this time—and what she was getting me into.

I drank up, my eyes fixed on the manila and my thoughts on what might lay ahead. Damn, I knew I'd regret it. I grabbed it and stuffed it into my inside jacket pocket. It weighed heavy as I drove home. I threw my jacket over a chair back, flopped into my armchair, and loosened my tie some more.

I dropped Maria's envelope on the coffee table. I watched it for a while. It didn't move. It looked plump and inviting. I picked it up and turned it over in my hands a few times. I knew I was going to open it. Sighing, I ripped the fold and looked inside. Cash. But I knew that already. More Benjamins gazed up at me. I was starting to build a collection.

There was something else in there. I emptied it out onto the coffee table. The hundreds, a gold-edged, high-quality card, and a flimsy piece of black material. I didn't touch them. Did I want to play these games?

Oh, what the hell? I lifted a corner of the cloth. It unfolded and hung like a guilty stain. A black strip of silky material with fastening strings and eye-holes. A Zorro mask. A robber's mask. A Mansion dungeon mask.

Private vices.

The card was an invitation to the Mansion. There was no address. If you didn't know where it was, you didn't get to go. The member inviting me was Miss Maria Delgado. The guest's name was Lance Lake. She never forgot to remind me of our first meeting.

I guess she had a trace of romance in her heart, somewhere.

8. BURNED IMAGES

I remembered again that Harry'd mentioned the Mansion. I thought of all the things I knew about the place and how I didn't like any of them. I gave him a call. It took him a while to pick up.

He didn't sound happy to hear my voice. "Got a client here, pal. Can it wait?"

I pressed on. "Remember the photo? The one you copied? Yes, I got the copies, thanks. Listen, you said you thought I was doing some work linked to the Mansion. What made you say that?"

"The wallpaper. Reminded me of the place you just mentioned. Looks the same."

Wallpaper! That confirmed it. "Don't tell me you're a member there?"

"Don't I wish? Need more cash than I can squeeze out of silver chloride, pal. Did some developing and blow-ups a while back for someone. Same wallpaper. She mentioned they were taken there then clammed up. You're not the only player in town, pal. There are other people can take candid photos, you know?" He was rambling, distracted. "These new little pocket-sized 35mm jobs really make it easier. Anyway, your snap reminded me of it."

Harry had a good eye for detail, in closeup.

"This client of yours—blonde, tall, dressed to kill, a ballbuster?"

"Heh! Maybe not so tall, but to die for? Sure. And dressed real classy. I knew her from somewhere..." His voice changed, got louder. "Be with you in a minute. Almost done."

I wasn't the only PI in town. Harry wasn't the only photo guy in town. I didn't look a gift coincidence in the mouth, but this one was hinky. A classy blond broad with links to the Mansion talking to a guy I just happened to play cards with and who maybe just happened to turn up later at my door? When things were too good to be true, I asked questions.

"Did you recommend me?"

"For what?"

"Don't play games, Harry."

"Honestly, pal. She didn't ask, and I didn't offer. Seemed she'd gotten someone to do her legwork already. You know, the photos. So I didn't give her your card. It's still on my pinboard by the door." He'd started to sound agitated.

"Pinboard? Listen, did you keep any copies of her photos? Any I could see?"

"Well...no, I couldn't. I mean, I didn't. You know I never—"

"Get them ready. I'm coming over."

"Wait, I have to ask—" His voice became muffled. He'd covered the mouthpiece.

"Harry, who's there with you? Who is it? Harry? Just hold on till I get there. Hear me? Harry?"

The line went dead.

———

The fire trucks beat me to Harry's place.

His home was no longer a house. It was a bonfire. The fire crews couldn't do anything to save it. They were just damping down the flames to stop them spreading in the evening breeze to the other houses on the street. Old, untreated clapboard was just firewood.

People get fascinated by car crashes and burning buildings, so there was a small crowd. There were a couple of fire department vehicles. There was an ambulance. There were two patrol cars and a couple of uniforms pretending to hold back a crowd that wasn't going anywhere near those flames. I spotted a face in the crowd, one I recognized from the library and the Hollywood Roosevelt lobby. Rusty hair and loud tie. Helluva coincidence. But I had other priorities right then.

I crossed the street to the ambulance. No one stopped me. Inside, a human shape under a blanket and the harsh stink of woodsmoke and chemicals and charred flesh reminded me of flamethrowers in a German forest.

Goodbye, Harry.

"Now, would he have been a friend of yours?" It was a New York Irish lilt, coming from behind me. I knew the voice. Sgt. Finegal Flynn. Big and brawny, he'd transferred from New York's finest when he got squeamish about some of their methods. He'd worked Bayville deputy for a while then transferred to LAPD. He found things pretty much the same here as back east. So he'd decided to blend in with as low a profile as his bulk could manage. He was on the city force now but still ran errands for Bayville's tin star in his trademark raincoat. We went back a long way, but I never forgot he was Sheriff Jackson's man in movietown.

I didn't bother turning. "Yeah. A friend."

"So would you be arriving conveniently just after the event or coming back after something you left in the building?"

"We play poker. We arranged a while ago to meet." Both statements were true.

"So that'd be just the two of you, then?"

"Yeah. Friendly game. What happened?"

He moved around to my left. Now he could see my face better. "Big explosion. House went up like tinder in minutes. Neighbors say he kept a mess of chemicals in the back room. Pretty much all over before the trucks got here. Know anything about it?"

I shook my head. It was simpler. "He smoked." It sounded vague enough.

"Yeah. Sounds good. Smoking near chemicals. Crazy as a rooster." He made a note in his little book. "Are all your friends crazy? Or just the ones who end up in the morgue?"

I ignored his jibe about events long past and best forgotten.

Smoking near chemicals? That wasn't Harry. He was too careful. But not careful enough about whoever was there when I called. Or should it be "whomever"?

Flynn was speaking. "They found him on the lawn. Crawled out on his arms, so he did. Neighbors say he needed a wheelchair?"

I nodded. "Anyone else in the house?"

"Not that we found yet. Neighbors saw nothing, as usual." His eyes narrowed. It wasn't a pleasant sight. "Whaddya mean 'anyone else'? Who else were you expecting at this game for two?"

"Just a few Kings and Queens."

Flynn moved closer, spoke in a confidential voice. "Play it that way if you want. But it looks like people around youse starting to suffer your bad luck again." He always had to dig up a past I wanted to forget. "One day, it'll be you flat on your back under a blanket in a meat wagon. Take my advice about who you're mixing with."

Now, who could he be talking about?

"If you can't mix a good cocktail, stay outta the kitchen." Flynn mangled metaphors like he was chewing nuts. Made me want to ram a dictionary down his throat.

He'd finished with me. He turned away, calling back over his shoulder. "Oh, and you know the drill?"

"Yeah. Don't leave town."

"To be sure, the boyyo's on fire tonight." His voice faded as he walked away, leaving his remark drifting like smoke on the wind.

9. RAKING OVER THE ASHES

Suddenly and briefly, business got brisk for a few days. In the morning, a shabby and pathetic middle-aged guy rambled on about his father's will he wanted me to chase up. He'd been excluded, wanted to know if it was true and why. I told him to see a lawyer. He insisted I help him. I took the job, mainly to get rid of him. I had too many distractions but also a lot of bills, despite Lyra's advance.

Still, I drove over and checked at the Orange County courthouse. Sure enough, he wasn't included. He could have looked for himself. I gave him the bad news over the phone. He actually sobbed, told me he was deep in debt, and poured out all his bad luck story. Of course, he wanted to know why he'd been cut out. I wanted to suggest seeing a medium but held off. He was in no state for that. I waived my fee and hoped he wouldn't call back.

Then there was a sobbing, middle-aged woman wanting me to find out if her husband's bowling night was spent actually bowling. I spent the next evening hanging around an echoing alley, listening to the rumbling of the lanes, the rattle of the pins, and the bowlers' cheers and howls. But no husband. She came back next day for my report. It wasn't good enough. She wanted to know where he actually was, in some desperate, masochistic way seeking something that would deepen her pain. I agreed to follow him the next week, just to put off the inevitable. She clasped my hand in both of hers, willing me with her eyes to find out the truth.

Sometimes I hate this job.

———

The church where they held Harry's funeral ceremony was gloomy. They always were. It was way too big for today's congregation. They always were at funerals. I brought white lilies.

I looked around at the gathered cardsharps: the cub reporter, the ex-cop, the jobless guy who always had cash…gambling buddies.

No family showed up. I didn't know if he had any still living. My ignorance made me feel guilty. I also didn't know who paid for the funeral. I didn't feel like poking my nose in.

A couple of strangers huddled in their own pew, keeping themselves to themselves. Someone said they were from his old FBI lab.

No official Bureau representative. That left a bad taste. He'd been one of their heroes, wounded in action and crippled. I saw Special Agent Dutch's name on a bunch of flowers. Flowers and a simple card. Real caring.

The priest droned on, sounding off catchall niceties for someone he never knew and now never would.

My mind wandered. Did any of our card game pals put Lyra onto Harry and me? I'd ask later. Now wasn't the time, and there'd be no game for a while. It'd have to wait.

Someone had told Lyra I was discrete. Someone. I guess it could be any ex-client, but I didn't get many clients in her class, the sort of people she'd mix with, these people she told me she could trust. I wondered who she *did* mix with. Maybe I should get to know more about Lyra?

I smothered a curse word—I was in church. But I'd been looking for the wrong person in those society pages. I should have been looking for Lyra. That's what Verity had said. Damn that woman! Damn them both. I couldn't get Jimmy's Bar out of my mind.

And I was sure Harry's death had to do with my case.

Sure, I'd chosen to take the risk when I guessed Lyra's missing man might be dangerous. But it was my risk, not Harry's. Who else would get hurt before this was over?

I should've dropped the case right then and walked away before anyone else got hurt. But this wasn't just a job anymore.

I decided to go see Dutch.

————

The Bureau building was pretty much the way I remembered it. Unimpressive. It sat back from a busy downtown street. Two stories, a few guys in dark suits, neat hair, distracted people chasing something or other with intensity and a handful of paperwork. I found my way to his office. The door was open, so I walked right in.

Special Agent John Deutsch was also little changed. Late twenties, square jaw, pale blue eyes, blond, the frame of a college football player not yet going to fat. His dark suit jacket hung over his chair, and his white shirt gleamed. He'd look good in a black uniform; he'd have fitted in well on the other side in the war. But he'd been on our side. So we called him "Dutch." He still displayed his college team photos and trophies around the room. On his desk—touchingly—was a picture of his wife and kids, a picture from which he was absent.

Dutch had been a rookie when the war began and just picked up where he left off after he came home. Some guys got all the luck.

He smiled his easy smile and crossed from his desk toward

me. "Hey, good to see you, Sarge. Long time. Come on in." There was no offered handshake.

"Stick to Corporal. It was a field promotion, and I got busted, remember? Covering for you got me busted."

"Yeah…" He was all smiles. "I remember we went on a bender when you got outta the field hospital, after the ambush in the forest—"

"I remember." My tone drew him up short.

He went quiet, avoiding my eyes, looking at his shoes. "Yeah. Rico. I forgot. Flamethrowers. Sorry."

Dutch passed me by, glanced up and down the hallway before closing the door, and only then squeezed my hand in a firm grip.

"Office problems?"

"No, no. Not really. Just privacy." He sounded a little hurried in his reassurance. "And as I remember it, you got *yourself* busted. You just won't let that go." His chuckle sounded forced. "Pull up a seat."

I slumped into the visitor chair and changed the subject. "So how's Lilly and the kids?"

He said they were fine, the kids doing well at school, and the usual meaningless updates. We chatted about general stuff for a while: the war years, old buddies, old adventures. I avoided mention of his Latina lady friend. Finally, he leaned forward and became serious. "But I guess you're here about Harry. Business or friendship?"

"I saw your flowers. Always wondered why you dropped out of the poker nights. You said it was family."

He looked uncomfortable and scratched the back of his neck. "Look, Harry was a good Bureau guy. We were good buddies before the shooting. But in recent years, he'd wandered into— shall we say—part-time work we can't be associated with."

I nodded. "At least, not officially. Were you warned off the funeral?"

"Hey, you know how it goes." He gave one of those open-armed, generous and empty shrugs that were supposed to gather sympathy and understanding but explained nothing. "But I couldn't just let him go without a few flowers. He was a good guy."

"So the Bureau had no interest in him anymore?" The point felt like it needed pursuing.

"Officially? No. Unofficially? Not that I know of." His steady gaze showed either honesty or surprisingly good acting. I couldn't tell which, but his sudden stillness was supposed to show sincerity. "Look, why all these questions?"

"Harry was murdered. I want to find out who did it."

He looked pained. "The report said accidental death. There's nothing to find out. Let it go."

"You telling me officially? What if I asked about the Mansion?"

His back stiffened, and he looked down, finding something interesting on his desk. "What if I hope you don't ask?"

"You got a problem with the Mansion?"

"See? You're asking." And then in a subdued voice, to himself, "The flowers' card was a mistake. I forgot you'd be there. You just won't let go of things."

There was a long silence. I used it to pressure him; he used it to resist.

He broke first. "Look, your file is clean right now. Don't go messing up."

"I still have a file?"

"Forever."

"But it's clean, eh? Officially? Or unofficially?"

"Officially. I kept you out of the Senator Booth shooting business, Sarge. Remember?"

"Just like I kept my mouth shut about the Feds' involvement."

That went down well. "Look, I'll say it again. You're clean right now. Don't go messing it up." He stood. I didn't.

"So I'm not being tailed by a redheaded guy with a lousy taste in ties?"

His bland smile slipped a little. "No idea who that might be. Hey, this was a great chat. Glad you dropped by, but I do have work to do. Oh, and maybe it's best if you don't drop in at the office again. You know how it is." He threw me what he must've thought was a sympathy-seeking grin. "But we should grab a beer sometime." He tried to sound enthusiastic. I hoped this jerk never went undercover.

"I'm getting the picture. Soon?"

"Well…" Again, that neck scratching. "Kinda busy right now, work, family, you know? Maybe in a few weeks?"

"Sure. Work, family. A few weeks. You'll call me, yeah?" I stood to go.

"Will do!" His smile returned as he showed me to the door. "See you around."

"Sure, see you 'round."

He rested his hand on my back as he eased me out the door, again looking up and down the hallway. As if no one in this cramped space hadn't pegged me already. Not too smart, old Dutch. Lots of guys like him on the government payroll.

———

I went back to the library, chasing down a thought.

I found Miss Grey rolling a trolley half-full of old dailies and magazines in a remote alleyway between shelves.

"Oh! You surprised me." There was a slight flush to her face. It must have been the surprise. "Just catching up with some filing." She gestured vaguely at the trolley. "You are becoming one of our biggest customers." She chuckled at her own joke, a chuckle full of nerves. "What can I do for you today?"

"Ever heard of a place called 'Catcher of Fog Dreams'? It's a small bay about twenty minutes' drive north of Santa Monica…I don't really remember." It was the first sign of my uncertainties as if the whole incident wasn't doubt enough of my sanity. My memory of that night was getting foggier. "Not really sure…"

"That would be in the 'Geography, Local, Maps' section." She looked disappointed. "Second floor," she explained.

"Oh, yes. I remember." I felt a twinge of disappointment myself.

"But if you're not in a hurry, I could look it up for you on my break." She offered so brightly, smiling with those big, puppy brown eyes of hers.

"That would be most kind of you, Miss Grey." Now why was I being so formal?

"I could give you a call if I find anything. If you leave me your number?"

She was wasted in this dusty place of the past. Of course, I would leave my number but not my business card with my profession blazing across it. Somehow, with those clean, innocent eyes on me, my profession made me feel dirty. I didn't come across innocence much in my world.

I scribbled the number on a piece of library header paper and handed it to her. She took it carefully with both hands, folding it once, twice, and slipping it in her bag. I imagined her holding it to her heart in the privacy of the archives' shelving. Just my little fantasy.

But she was a sweet kid.

10. CATCHING DREAMS

Miss Grey called me at home next day. It was a Saturday. She was real eager, said she wanted to show me something. I drove straight over to the library.

"Come and see!" She took my arm and led me to a reading table. I enjoyed the experience. A huge book of maps lay open, ready.

She started explaining. "I couldn't find anything with that name, so I looked up the Spanish translation. I surmised that the first settlers might have renamed it and there was a chance they'd simply converted the original name."

She actually said "surmised." Ten-dollar words just seemed to roll off her tongue naturally. Once again, I felt cheap.

"I didn't find anything at first, so I played around with the words a bit, like a crossword puzzle."

I'd heard of crosswords. Saw one in the *LA Times*. Made no sense to me. I nodded.

"And I found this." She pointed. I peered.

The map showed a small curving bay with rocky cliffs to the south and a lighthouse to the north on a small finger of rock poking out accusingly at Japan. The label read *"Bahía de los sueños."*

"Bay of Dreams," she translated for me.

It fit. I almost hugged her. Instead, I bent lower, looking closer. She did the same, until our heads were almost touching. I noticed her perfume, something light and fresh. I wanted to say something nice. Instead, I pulled my head back a little and kept quiet.

There was no road marked, which didn't surprise me. It wouldn't have been worth marking, a dirt road going nowhere.

Something dark inside me lightened. That strange evening hadn't been a total illusion—not a *total* illusion. "You really are something special, Miss Grey." She smiled at the appreciation. At least I knew the geography wasn't a dream. "Now how about the bar license?"

"I checked the liquor license registry. There was nothing listed for that name, or anything related, going back ten years."

I looked around. "Since when was the register kept in the library?"

She looked down briefly then back up at me. The tip of her tongue showed briefly as she licked her lips. "It's not. I know someone at the department, and he looked for me."

"On a Saturday?" I tried to make it sound good-natured, but something was wrong here.

She paused for the briefest of moments, holding my eyes in a steady gaze. "I rang and asked yesterday." She tensed with a touch of hostility in her voice. "You can go look for yourself if you don't—"

"Whoa! I believe you. Just pleased you have such good connections. I'm really very grateful."

My grin was genuine. She'd given me what I needed.

She relaxed, gave me the warmest of smiles. Miss Grey had made my day, and knowing that had made *her* day. I felt I owed her dinner, at least. But I pushed the thought back for another time. I already had too many dames on my mind right then.

So Jimmy's Bar wasn't listed. I guessed I knew it wouldn't be.

It could just be an old speakeasy keeping up its old habits. Jimmy, or whoever he was, had said the bar had been there a long time. It was certainly well hidden. And it looked old. A speakeasy would explain a lot. And bathtub booze might explain the dream.

Even so, the Twenty-first Amendment was passed nearly twenty years ago. Speakeasies were long gone with Prohibition, thank God. That was a long time to hide. But there were too many puzzles to do with that night.

I knew I'd have to go back, to see if there really was a bar there or if the whole thing was just a dream. I needed to know if I could trust my memory.

The uncertainty still needled me. Mom's doctors said sufferers could get hallucinations, but they didn't know much about how her illness worked. She'd certainly started having them, smelling perfume, seeing ghosts… But I must have been a long way from that stage, even if I had it. I didn't want to ask Miss Grey for information, to expose a possible weakness in myself. Not this time. Maybe another time.

I asked her about something else. "One more thing. I saw a ring, a circle about a foot across, dressed with feathers. Know what that is?"

"Oh, it sounds like a dreamcatcher." She had my full attention. "Is it connected with the *Bahía de los sueños*?" She said it like she spoke Spanish every day.

I wondered how much I should share. I didn't want her thinking I was crazy. That seemed important, somehow.

She was answering her own question. "No, of course, it wouldn't be connected. They were used by the tribes in Canada and the northeast areas. Perhaps some plains tribes, I'd have to check. But none around here."

"Keep talking."

"Indians believed that if you hung one over the head of a sleeper, it would catch nightmares, bad dreams. I think they were used mostly for children, as adults needed to have dreams, good and bad, so they could interpret them. According to Dr. Freud—"

"So if I saw one here on the coast, it would be a fake?"

"Well, perhaps not a fake. It could be a souvenir from someone's travels or belong to a soldier who settled here after the Indian wars. Did someone try to sell you one?"

"No, I just saw it and wondered what it was. Dreamcatcher, huh?" I kept wondering how much of Jimmy's Bar was real and how much was fake. If it even existed. But how could I imagine things like the dreamcatcher when I'd never seen one?

This was burning up too much thinking time. I should be focusing on the Lyra business. But I had to go back, to find out what Jimmy's bar was all about and who this Verity was. But that would have to wait for Sunday, for tomorrow.

———

Back home, Maria's invitation still lay on the coffee table next to the empty Scotch bottle and the overflowing ashtray.

I changed into my new monkey suit. I felt like some cheap hick in a brand-new tux that hadn't been trained to sit well on him. Real clients would have comfortable, old family heirloom tuxes that fit well after years of training and still looked new. Mine was just a newborn pup. I shrugged and turned to the full-length mirror in my closet door.

The reflection told a different tale. I guessed anyone looked good in an expensive tux and a fresh haircut. I sure did.

Fastening the bow tie darkened my mood. I needed an extra pair of hands. I guess that's one of the reasons rich guys have starlets around them.

I drained my tumbler, grabbed my smokes and the invitation. I left my ID and holster on the dresser. I didn't want some doorman goon finding them and asking dumb questions. But I felt naked without them.

Twilight was looming. I couldn't delay any longer.

11. THE MANSION

I knew the way.

I drove north and west, past the well-behaved houses of the poor and the middle-rich, through the neat avenues of Beverly Hills, and on into the countryside. I thought over the sticky webs I'd gotten tangled in before with the Mob, the moneyed, and the movietown folk associated with the Mansion. I still wasn't convinced this visit was wise. But it was under new management, so maybe it wouldn't be so bad.

The asphalt paving petered out into a dust road. The road signs petered out, too. No one came to the Mansion who didn't know where they were going. The track led up to heavy iron gates set in a high stone wall.

The acrid stench of moneyed privilege hit me as the scowling gate guards checked my invitation. Their snarling German Shepherds were even less welcoming. The guards waved me through, the hounds lunging at my car, jaws wide and slobbering, leashes straining. Dogs just didn't like me, or maybe these monsters hated everyone. I flinched even though the windows were wound up tight. The long scars on my forearm tingled the way they always did when I saw Shepherds. My finger itched to pump two down each canine throat—one for the kill, one for revenge.

Now I could see the main building, surrounded by acres of lawn. It looked like something dragged across from Olde England via a Hollywood designer's nightmares. Reminded me of Greystone Mansion. I'd never entered through the Mansion's front door, but I'd expect Boris Karloff to be filling in as butler, adding a touch of cheer to the welcome. There was a fountain in the wide, graveled area in the front. A cute, naked cherub spouted water from a jar into a circular pool. The welcoming light above the doorway would show the guards who wanted in. Otherwise, the dozens of windows were shaded, appropriately dark and gloomy.

I passed a fleet of parked cars, mostly big enough to fit my apartment in the trunk. I kept going till I reached some big trees, oaks maybe, at the side of the building. They hid my old wheels from view. In the moonlight, I'd counted a few expensive rides, all neatly lined up. A few fancy Italian sports models were parked more informally. Rich youngbloods scattering Daddy's cash around, I guessed. The sons of the rich always chose to be difficult.

To one side, a cluster of chauffeurs was marked by the occasional flare of a lighter and the burning ends of their smokes. I imagined them eyeballing my wheels in disgust as I'd passed. Still, it was a fine night. They were happy to be with their own kind. Lucky guys.

My feet crunched on the gravel as I headed for the entrance, a heavy wooden double door with a neat peaked arch. There was a fancy speakeasy grille in one door.

Sadly, it was not Mr. Karloff who opened the door. Someone had been watching my approach and swung the door open as I got close. Impressive timing. A frail-looking old geezer in butler costume, tails and all, stood in the revealed entryway. Two other guys, less frail-looking, stood not very discretely back a few paces. Blank-faced gorillas all done up in tuxes. Lots of old, dark wood lined the walls.

"Good evening, sir." The old guy greeted me, somehow deferential yet superior at the same time. Maybe he'd smelled the brand-newness of my tux. Anyway, he sure sounded British English to me. I'd not met any butlers when my unit was stationed in England in the run-up to D-Day, but I knew from the movies what they sounded like. I guessed when you're rich enough, you could afford an original.

I dug out the invitation and offered it. He didn't touch it. He glanced at the name and date, gave a slight sniff, then stood back and gestured in a wide sweep of his arm toward the hallway beyond.

"Welcome, Mr. Lake. I wish you an enjoyable and profitable evening." It was a routine doorman's greeting, but he'd injected the sparkle of class.

"Thank you, James." He didn't blink at the cliché. I hesitated at the entrance.

"Your first visit, sir? Mr. Martino will show you the way." He didn't quite snap his fingers, but one of the goons behind him shuffled into motion along the hallway without a word. I liked the old geezer. Looked like he enjoyed his almost-top-of-the-heap position just below the owners.

"Thanks again, James." My hand moved to my wallet pocket. I was used to tipping doormen, even when they earned more than I did.

His gaze followed the action. He spoke without a trace of contempt. "That will not be necessary, Mr. Lake. And the name is Henry, if you require any further assistance." A slight bow of the head, the slightest hint of a warm smile. Deferential and superior. I felt put in my place without any malice.

I threw him a friendly grin as I strolled off behind the Martino gorilla. He ambled past doors on the right and left, heading for the great double doors squatting between great twin sweeps of matching staircases up to the balcony above. I heard a vague rumble and clatter with a hint of cool saxophone as I got nearer. He opened the door and stepped back, real polite, blank faced, and a gust of noise hit me. Those doors were pretty thick to smother all that sound.

It was the casino. A small jazz combo was playing a smooth and soft version of "Got You Under My Skin" in the background as white balls rattled around their wheels and croupiers at a half-dozen card tables murmured to the high -rollers gathered around the baize. Through the smoke haze, jewelry sparkled like it belonged with the vast chandeliers hanging above. Shrill, female voices rose above the hubbub. I felt the doors close behind me, and some smiling floozy in a waitress costume like Maria's wiggled toward me on her heels, a tray of drinks on offer.

I needed one. I took a tall glass of bubbles. It was quality stuff. Her fixed smile didn't slip as she shimmied away in search of new saps to soften up with alcohol.

My first glance around the room convinced me I would have been happier with the chauffeurs. Big money, old money, new money. Movie money, booze-and-girls money, nose candy money, political money. And all the arm candy a man could want.

I recognized a few faces from the big screen or the gossip columns, especially those I'd been eyeballing recently. I guessed most of the others were on the news pages I didn't read or were important enough to not get photographed by the press at all.

Not getting photographed? Now, *that* rang a bell.

I pulled out a Lucky from the pack, which stayed in my pocket. I didn't own a gold cigarette case and didn't want to play sore thumb. Behind me, someone spoke a familiar name I almost didn't react to.

"Mr. Lake?" It was an educated voice, with a mocking edge to its East Coast twang. I turned to see. Middle-aged and trim, wearing a full head of chestnut hair. "I'd like to welcome you to our little club." His smile was blandly pleasant, but I felt his eyes on me.

"Well, thank you. I didn't catch your name."

He gave me an old-fashioned look. "And I only caught the name on your invitation, Mr. Lake."

"Touché." I raised my glass to him.

"It is customary for invitees to accompany their guests on their first visit, but I understand your 'Guinevere' is…occupied, at present. I trust you will be patient. Or I can find you another escort for tonight? If not, please feel at liberty to wander the room until she is available. Oh, and will you be exploring the basement areas? I can provide a mask if you require one. Miss Delgado usually provides them in advance for her first-timers."

"Not tonight, thank you." I tried to hide my gut reaction. I didn't like his tone of voice when he spoke about Maria. He withdrew graciously and kept only a distant eye on me as I strolled around. I watched some guy lose and another win, but most of the chips steadily drifted toward the croupiers and dealers. I noticed a couple of women in men's tuxes, faces I knew from the big screen, standing very close together. No one else seemed to notice or care, but it disturbed me in some pleasant way.

And suddenly, there was Maria. She was the cat's meow. I'd never seen her look so good or wearing so much money. Dolled up to die for in a red evening dress, elegant, but simple enough to keep your eyes on the contents. Not a waitress, tonight. Perhaps not a waitress any night, not anymore. At least, that's what the lackey had implied.

I'd never wanted to ask what she did these days.

She prowled with her cat's sway toward me and straight into my arms. It felt good. Damn good. But too damn brief.

12. RAISING THE STAKES

For a while, I forgot all the dark stuff. I inhaled her heady scent, felt her soft satin skin against my face and her body pressed against mine.

Then she stepped back. The magic moment broke.

I took her bare arms in a gentle grip and held her still so I could examine her face. Too much face powder and eyeshadow. Still hiding the remains of the hotel bruising, I guessed.

She saw my look and turned away, stepping back out of my grasp, gesturing vaguely around the room. "You ever been here before?" It sounded like a natural question, but I knew she was just dodging any question I might have asked.

"I don't gamble." Yeah, I could duck questions, too.

She raised an eyebrow.

"Okay, I play a little friendly poker, but I don't play for these stakes."

"Cheapskate. I should get me more rich friends."

I reached out and touched the fine fabric of her dress with my fingertips. "Looks like you have enough rich friends."

The blood red of Maria's gown highlighted her dark skin and long, glossy black hair shining in the lighting.

"You like?" Hands on hips, she turned her body this way and that for inspection.

"I don't like what goes on in the nose candy factory in the basement. You know they supply half of movietown? And for reasons I can guess, the Feds and the LAPD are hands off."

"I like hands off." She smiled that heart-aching smile of hers. "Sometimes."

"And for another, I don't like the other setup in the basement. The one you need a fancy mask for."

"What *do* you mean, Sir Lancelot?" She threw me an exaggerated astonishment. "Just a few games. *We* play games, you and me. You don't like games?" She pouted. Back into teasing mode.

"Not those kinds of games."

"Okay, so no tour tonight." Back came her scowl. "I'll go find Isabella. Wait here."

"Remind me why she can't come to my office?"

"You crazy. She wants to size you first. And your office isn't private."

"Size me up, you mean? And..." I glanced around the massed gamblers and service staff. "Here is private?"

Her scowl deepened. "Wait here. Might take a few minutes." She prowled off in her expensive outfit.

As I enjoyed the free champagne, I scanned the crowd again, playing spot the movie star. I was also looking for a ginger-haired guy, wondering if his bow tie would be as tasteless as the patterned horrors he usually wore.

I didn't find him, but across the room, I spotted a shade of blonde I recognized. I weighed it up a little then decided. I weaved my way through the tables toward her until I stood right behind her. She wore a figure-hugging white gown with cross-straps across her naked back. It was a nice view. She was watching some guy throw away his money at the craps table. She turned to whisper something to him, and I caught a view of that immaculate profile. He held up his dice and asked her to blow on them. She smiled a melting smile, her eyelids closing slowly as if she was seducing the dice.

I didn't know how the dice felt about it, but it got to me.

"Lyra?"

She stiffened and turned to face me, recovering her poise. "Good evening. I did not expect to see you here."

"I can tell. Why not?"

"I thought it would be…"

"Out of my class?"

"Not to your taste."

I shrugged. She whispered to the gambler then took my arm, drawing me into a secluded corner. I don't like having my back to the room, but I guessed nothing bad would happen to me with so many witnesses.

"Are you here to pursue my inquiry?"

"I'm here for work, not for pleasure." It was strictly true. Maria wanted me to investigate something, and I hated the place.

She released my arm, stepping back to appraise me, her head cocked on one side. "Well, you have done much better than I thought."

I took it as a compliment.

She didn't intend it to be one. "Have you been to Tahoe yet?"

I waited until a wandering cocktail waitress had passed by. "Not yet."

She frowned as she considered that. I pressed my advantage. "You never said who recommended me. Someone from this place?"

A cold front passed over her face. We were back to the reluctant routine. "In a way. Indirectly." She cocked her head as if a thought had suddenly struck her. She examined my face, and her expression changed to puzzlement then realization. "You don't know who he is, do you? You don't know about Tahoe." Her glare launched a blast of icy Alaskan air at me. "Why exactly are you here?" It wasn't a question, more like a demand.

"I told you, I'm working." Now it was my turn to do some arm grabbing. "We have to meet. And talk. Seriously talk."

I felt her whiplash scowl again. "Remove. Your. Hand."

I stared into her eyes and tightened my grip. "We. Have. To. Talk."

She cocked her head and reconsidered me. Her eyes softened. She spoke as if she was rewarding me. "I shall call at your office on Monday morning." Her gaze drifted to a point somewhere behind me, over my left shoulder. She nodded to someone. "I have to go now." She glanced down at my hand and back at my face. I released her and watched her strut her way back to the money man without a backward glance at me.

So now I knew where my client spent her evenings, the kind of people she mixed with, and probably where her guy had been spotted. Harry had been right. And that was no thanks to Lyra. Was she working here? Was she a freelancer? Or someone's date? Hard to tell without asking for a set of rules or her membership details. It was good to know my original assessment wasn't far wrong. I still only had some background, but it was a start point. Did I want to chase it? I owed her some time, and I was curious. Mostly I wanted to know about her and Harry and who killed him. To her, it was some kind of a game. I decided to play.

Now, what did that Tahoe reference mean?

Waiting for Maria, I watched Lyra whispering in the gambler's ear, playing with a lock of his hair, stroking and kissing the back of his neck, seducing him right there in the huddle around the crap tables. I didn't enjoy the stirrings inside me. I had to look away.

Maria entered my line of sight with a pretty Hispanic girl in tow. She looked too young even for this place. Subdued, no sparkle. She wore green. Green didn't suit her.

"Here he is, Isabella. We take a table. Come." Maria dragged her friend past me and through an archway into a smaller room with a bar on the far wall, a scattering of patrons, and two waitresses in the cigarette-girl outfits.

She headed for a corner table some way from its neighbors. I trailed along behind, surrendering to the situation, for now, letting Maria take the lead in what was to come.

A waitress appeared as we took our seats. We ordered drinks, and Maria gave some hand signal I guessed meant she was paying. We waited in silence, Isabella's gaze flickering all over my face. She noticed me watching her watching me, and she lowered her eyes to the table between us until the waitress had delivered our drinks.

"Tell me again why we had to meet here. Why not in some hotel foyer or at your apartment? Most of all, why she couldn't come to my office?"

"You needed to see the place. Don't scowl at me. This is my *territorio*. You don't live highlife. You needed to see, to taste this good life here, no? And now you've seen and tasted, isn't it better than your crummy job?"

I kept scowling.

Maria ignored it, turning instead to the girl. "Her sister's gone missing. Tell him."

Isabella showed her reluctance to talk, hunched up, avoiding my eyes. Maria encouraged her in a rapid Spanish. I only caught a few of the words, but it was clear she was bullying the younger girl. I lit a Lucky and enjoyed sipping my drink while I waited, occasionally glancing around the room, spotting famous faces, admiring the gowns and the waitresses.

Once my glass was empty, I shuffled in my seat and scraped the chair backward, preparing to stand. Isabella finally glared at me and began to speak. It was almost a whisper, heavily accented, and hard to hear above the background noise. But I gathered enough to put together her story.

Yes, I was hearing another story.

Hers was about her little sister, Bonita. A timid girl, she'd followed Isabella to this wonderful paradise. The sisters never did any "such work," as she called it, casting a guilty look at Maria, who patted her hand and urged her to continue.

They'd been waitresses who encouraged the patrons to buy champagne while they just smiled and looked pretty. But no "such work," she assured me again.

The boss, Caldera, had taken a fancy to Bonita. She quickly became his favorite. "Going on dates," she'd said. Isabella had protested, but this just threw the sisters apart. She started staying at the Mansion after work, seeing less and less of Isabella. She'd grown pale and distracted. She took to wearing long sleeves; Isabella exposed her own arm. I understood. No needle marks. "She no listen. I want to take her home, away from this place, but she no listen. Say she in love, *Madre de Dios*! In love? And how the boss was big man. Powerful. Rich."

She said her sister had suddenly disappeared. "Not seen here for work. Not come home anymore."

Maria had asked after her at the Mansion but met a wall of silence.

"Something bad happen her. Here. In this place." She looked around the bar, and her fear showed. "I know it! So she hides now."

Something bad happened at the Mansion every day, but I said nothing.

"I want my little sister back. She hide, for shame. Maybe. Don't know. But I forgive. Forgive all. I just want find her and bring her to home to Mother. To get away this place."

I thought about it, listening to the gambling noises from the main room. Isabella was so young. Vulnerable. I needed to help her. But...I had to ask the obvious question. "I guess you can't talk to the police?" I already knew the answer.

"*Polizia*? No, no. *Hay Polizia. Federales*, no!" She panicked so much, Maria had to hold her still.

How come nobody ever wanted to talk to the cops? Yeah, I knew why. So many illegals.

I spoke quietly. "Maria, this is bad. Meeting here. Someone might know I'm a private investigator—"

Isabella's eyes opened wide, and her jaw fell open. She

turned on Maria, letting fly with a spitting, hissing outburst of Spanish. I glanced around. No one was paying any attention. Yet.

"*Madre de Dios.*" She crossed herself. "*Investigador privado*? Is same as cops." She turned her fiery gaze at Maria. "You say he a friend."

"He is. He is a friend. Tell her."

"Isabella, I *am* a friend. *Amigo.* Look, give me something to work on. Full name, photo, working name—" This drew another angry glare from Isabella. "Okay, forget it." I stood. The meeting was over.

Maria grabbed my arm with one hand and Isabella's with the other. She pulled me down and drew her friend close to her, whispering something in her ear I couldn't catch.

I pressed on. "Look, I'd have to ask around, people who knew her, people from here, other girls, management maybe." Again, Isabella's big eyes widened, flashing the whites of her eyes at me. "But you don't want me to do that. So I really don't know what I can do."

Maria took over. "The girls here won't talk. I should show you the basement so you know what happens to girls who cause trouble."

I really did not want to be shown the basement. "Rain check."

She touched a finger to my shirt, tracing a line on my chest, following the scar line she knew lay beneath. Those big, sad puppy eyes triggered bad memories. She knew all about Private Rico's broken-hearted sister, how I'd lied about a quick, painless death when I visited his family... She knew how to pull my strings. I cursed her silently. I also cursed myself for telling her too much about the scar and my nightmares.

I lifted her hand off my chest and moved it to her knee. I heard the weary resignation in my voice. "Just what do you want me to do?"

"To find her sister."

"I'm not a magician."

"You are the best." She hugged my arm, pressing my bicep against her firm breasts. I looked down into the dangerous dark pools of her eyes, thinking again how I could drown in them a happy man. "And," her voice went low, "I say a big thank you after. Yes?" Now she was all smiles.

I surrendered. I nodded, reassuring Isabella, satisfying Maria. I made a show of taking down some notes...

Another missing girl in movietown. She was an illegal, an addict, and a hooker. Hookers went missing in the big city. No one cared, least of all the cops. I knew in my heart she wasn't really hiding. Did I really want to find out what had happened to her? No snooping around at the Mansion, no cops...I had no idea where to start. This was becoming a familiar trap.

Dames as clients? Pains in the ass.

"Isabella is staying with me. You get something, you come by, okay?" She smiled a dark-eyed smile. "You remember where it is?"

As if I could forget. Even my car knew the best local parking spot.

As I strolled through the main casino room on my way out, I spotted the Martino thug paying me too much attention from across the room. I'd shaken off ginger boy, and now I had someone else watching me. I hoped the girls would be okay. Hope was all I had to offer them.

I was sure it wasn't going to be enough.

13. SUNDAY AT JIMMY'S BAR

I dreamed about a soft-spoken woman with her hand on my shoulder as the ocean's hypnotic lulling washed away the dirt of my job.

I woke to another Santa Ana September day. I didn't need to look at the clock to check the time; it was exactly the time for my first coffee and smoke of the day.

Halfway through my second cup, the fog lifted from my brain a little. It was Sunday, a good day to find Jimmy's Bar.

Things looked different in daylight. It was hard to find the dirt road turnoff. I nearly gave up. But I didn't. My car rolled down the sloping track, and this time, I could admire the view to my right.

Ocean. All I could see from the track was ocean. Even the lighthouse and the far cliffs were obscured by rocks and scruffy shrubs. Only after the last bend did the flat parking area and the rundown shack come into view.

There were no cars, as I'd expected. Jimmy's was closed. I hadn't expected that. Maybe I should have. It looked even more shabby in the daylight. Locked doors and storm-boarded windows. No friendly twinkle lights. They were there, hanging from the guttering, swaying a little in the breeze. Just not switched on.

I banged on the door and called out my hellos. No response. I tried to peer through any cracks in the window boards. No dice.

It's "no dice" when the bones couldn't be found.

I thought about it for a while or two, with the crash of waves and the screams of gulls keeping me company.

Well, there I was and there I'd come for a reason. I found a narrow path around the shack, partly blocked by thorny shrubs. My feet sank into the dry, soft sand, leaving a scuffling line of hollows that slowly filled up again. Maybe a sharp observer could see someone had passed this way. I couldn't cover my tracks. I wasn't sure why I'd want to.

And there it was: the jutting boardwalk, my chair and table at the end.

I left a trail of sand spilling from my pants' cuffs along the wooden flooring. The rear door was locked. The windows were closed up just like the front. So I headed out along the pier. I wondered if Verity had snuck round the side when she vanished —if she actually existed. I still wasn't convinced. Or maybe I was. If not, why was I there?

I eased down into the rickety chair, ignoring its creaking, and gazed out at the ocean to wait.

For what, I didn't know.

Out across the water, the gulls circled lazily in their noisy way, occasionally swooping down for something glittering below the water's surface. I guessed they were California gulls. I wasn't a bird expert. I had a client...said he was an ornithologist. A real nice guy who'd gotten too wrapped up in writing books, who spent too little time with his wife, who spent too much time with her neighbor. He gave me one of his books when he paid his bill. Said he didn't need it anymore. Shot himself next day. His cheating wife inherited not a lot as he'd invalidated his insurance by suiciding. It's a tough world.

I'd read anything. It passed the time. Especially when I was between receptionists.

Didn't remember much of what I read, though.

The Yurok Indians Jimmy'd claimed lived here once must have hunted the gulls.

Wished I'd brought the bird book with me.

I smoked a little, closed my eyes, waited. I listened to the ocean breathing and the gulls squawking.

A long time later, nothing had happened.

I cursed myself for a fool and tramped back the way I'd come, ignoring the gulls' mocking cries and leaving a pile of Lucky butts on the boards.

Half a pack, gone up in smoke that drifted away forever like a forgotten memory.

———

Monday. Late afternoon. I saw someone's vague outline through the outer office door's glass panel. I kept the inner door open when I was between receptionists. Was it Lyra? My brief stir of interest faded when I recognized the lumbering bulk.

"Do come in, Finflynn!"

"You ever gonna get tired of mocking my name? It's Sgt. Flynn to you." He ambled in, glancing around as if looking for someone to suspect of something. His wrinkled coat matched his world-weary face. "You alone?" It was his turn to joke.

"As you can see. Want a slug?" I pulled out a bottle and two glasses from the lockable drawer of my desk as he flopped into my visitor chair. He took off his fedora, revealing a shiny skull framed by a vanishing line of graying light brown hair.

"Don't mind if I do." He wiped his forehead on the back of his sleeve. "Such sticky days, this summer."

I didn't suggest he take his coat off. He never took it off. He rarely had it cleaned, either. "Social call? Or maybe you need some assistance with a tricky case? I'd like to have 'Consultant to the LAPD' on my business card."

"Cut the comedy."

"Okay. Is it about Harry?" He looked blank. "The fire the other night," I prompted.

"Oh, that? No. His cigarette set off his storeroom. Chemicals and stuff. Accident. Case closed. Body released. Weren't you at his funeral? Thought he was a friend."

I kept a blank face. Harry wasn't careless. And there'd been someone with him when I phoned. Maybe the visitor was the careless one? Or maybe the visitor had taken care of Harry. "So why do I have the pleasure of serving you drinks today?"

"Sheriff Jackson asked me to drop in and have a chat with you."

"You making house calls for the Bayville tin star?" I topped him off. It was good to keep the local constabulary happy. But not too happy. I had a bad reputation to keep up.

"It's about your license renewal." He downed the glass in one and held it out for more. I gave him a refill.

"It's valid for another few months. And Jackson doesn't issue investigator licenses for the city."

"True. But he knows the right people, can put a good word in for you." He looked over the rim of the tumbler as he made to toast me. His cheery voice turned dark. "Or a bad word."

I took the point. "Good of him to take such an interest in the voters. Election due?"

"Cut the snappy stuff. He's not sure you know who you're meddling with. Maybe you've gotten in a little above your depth."

"Am I supposed to know who I don't know I'm meddling with? Or does he want to keep me guessing?"

"I hear tell you ain't got a big client roster to consider. The message is just stick to straying husbands and dogs. Remember, a squeaky wheel gathers no moss." He stood. "And thanks for the Scotch. But I prefer Irish. That's whiskey with an 'e.' Remember for next time."

"There'll be a next time?"

"The way you play life like it's a casino, I do believe there will be." He replaced his hat, adjusted it to no visible improvement, and waddled out, leaving my door wide open.

I gazed at the shape vanishing down the hallway toward the stairwell. I watched until there was just empty space between me and the far wall.

Now, what the hell was *that* all about?

I'd waited for Lyra to show but no dice.

I decided to get out of this dump, to go see Mom, to get some fresh air and less-confusing conversation.

―――――

Mom wasn't so bright that day. We talked for a while. Or rather, *I* talked for a while. She nodded or smiled when she thought she should.

It was getting late, and she was getting tired. Then she kinda woke up.

She turned her head, looking around the room like she was searching for someone. She whispered something I couldn't make out. It sounded like a question, rising in tone at the end. I leaned in closer. "What is it, Mom?"

"I was looking for Verity. Where is she? I can smell her perfume again. And I saw her here a minute ago…"

I stared at her as ice water ran through my veins. "Verity?"

She nodded, still seeking out someone she couldn't see, pushing me feebly to one side to look behind me.

I was reluctant to ask, "Mom, who is Verity?"

"Oh, it was before…" She turned to face me as her voice trailed away. I saw those fierce, defiant eyes sparkling at me as the years fell away and she was whole again for a moment. She grasped my hand, clutched it tight, glanced furtively about the room, and leaned in closer. She placed a trembling finger against my lips. "Shh! Mustn't tell. Ever."

Then the spell broke. Her eyes glazed over, and her face muscles relaxed. "I want to sleep now. Before…" Her face turned even whiter, and she covered it with her hands.

"What is it, Mom?" I signaled an attendant for help.

She began to sob. "Oh, Verity, poor Verity. She died, you know? There was a fire. She died. My poor Verity…"

I patted her hand to comfort her as the attendant rushed over full of concern but throwing a scowl my way. Mom slowly calmed, and her habitual blank look spread across her features. Then another brief flare of awareness sparked. She smiled up at me from tired eyes and patted my hand.

"But you're a good man, son. Look after her. A good man…"

Vagueness grew in her eyes. "I'll be letting you go now."

14. LOOKING FOR TRUTH

Next morning, I went back to the retirement home. I wanted to dig for anything about mom's Verity, but her thoughts were somewhere else. She didn't even recognize me. She talked in her frail voice about the Midwest farm where she'd grown up, about friends and family from those days. People I'd never known and were probably mostly dead. But she spoke of them like they were still alive. She soon tired and couldn't get the words out. It was one of my more painful visits.

I'd asked to see her doctor but needed to go outside for a while, sitting on a wooden bench, smoking a Lucky or two to regain my balance.

A pretty nurse wearing perfect whites and a professional sympathetic expression came looking for me and took me to his office. A brass plate gave his name, followed by lots of initials. He offered a seat. I took it. He offered tea. I took it but didn't drink it. His office was bright and sunny, decorated with diplomas and photos of people shaking his hand. It inspired confidence and calm. I wondered where the photos of his wife and kids were.

He sat with his back to a large window overlooking the neat mown lawn to the rear of the building. The landscaped trees and bushes pretty much hid the high wall around the grounds. This was an expensive place. I had to assume these people were the best. I had no choice.

He clasped his hands on the desktop and gave me a bland smile. "How can I help? If it's about who set up the trust fund again…" He spread his hands in a gesture of honest helplessness. Clearly, he remembered our previous conversations about this.

"No, it's about symptoms."

"Very well. Shoot." He was smiling. Sounded like he'd read too many dime novels about PIs and wanted to make me feel at home.

I wasn't in the mood. I went straight to the point or, rather, almost to the point. "You said she might have hallucinations?"

He started to explain again how little was known about her illness. "But in some patients…" He lost me in seconds.

"So that's a possible 'yes'?"

He nodded, now wearing his serious face. "Possible. Yes. Such experiences could be genuine memories surfacing unexpectedly. It's all very uncertain. She might even experience things that aren't really happening." That fit Mom's claims about someone called Verity being in the lounge. But I didn't dare get tempted into thinking her Verity could be the same as mine. That way led to madness.

Now came the biggie. "Is it catching or hereditary?"

Something gave me away. He became reassuring. "You cannot catch it from a sufferer. Regarding heredity…" He pursed his lips, looked uncertain. "We are still researching. We still don't have much information. It is possible…" He gave me a long look then leaned forward, steepling his fingers. "Is this a chat about your mother, or is it a consultation?"

I hesitated.

"Don't worry about the fee." He was dismissive. "The trust will take care of it. Just tell me what's worrying you."

Fee? He'd misread me.

Then he misread my silence. "I assure you the illness is nothing to be ashamed of. Sometimes younger people do suffer the vagueness associated with the elderly. We don't know why, but in coming years—"

It tumbled out. It was my turn to tell my story. "Listen, I think I had a dream. I had a conversation with someone. Someone who claimed to be involved in a case I'm working on. But it was a dream. And her name was one Mom mentioned yesterday, claiming she was in the lounge with us, but who she said was dead." It sounded like rambling. I guess it was.

He leaned back and cocked his head. "The only connection was the name?"

"Well...it could be I dreamed it and Mom imagined the woman was here with me. So there's a connection...maybe?" I heard myself talking and realized what I sounded like. I shook my head and looked down at the carpet. "Yeah, it's crazy. Sorry to waste your time."

"You are not wasting my time at all." He looked me over like he was considering how to break bad news, tapping a finger against his lips. He leaned forward, resting his elbows on the desk and steepling his fingers again. "Memory is a strange thing. Perhaps your subconscious is confusing things. Perhaps you are remembering the events out of sequence." He paused again before continuing very cautiously. "I understand you saw action in Germany, were badly wounded..." He checked for my reaction. He was brave to continue. "Some soldiers suffer from what used to be called shell shock... You are always very tense, the way you hold yourself, the way you speak. Distress over your mother's decline cannot help that. I am not an expert in post-combat anxiety issues. Perhaps I could recommend someone?" He reached for the address book on his too-tidy desk.

I felt like someone was grinding sand into my brain. I stood, maybe too fast. "Thanks, Doc. I'll consider it."

We both knew I wouldn't.

Somehow, I found it easier to consult with Miss Grey.

———

"A stroke? You would like to know the symptoms? I don't know offhand, but I could do some research if you would like." Always generous, always on my side.

Hell, sometimes I wished she wasn't so... "I don't want to impose."

She laughed softly. I liked the way her eyes crinkled at the corners. "Oh, I have a surfeit of spare time. Archives is not the busiest of sections. And I can research things that interest me on my breaks. And my evenings..." She left it hanging. I chose not to bite.

"I'd be really grateful if you could." I wondered how grateful I would be. "But don't get into trouble for me."

"Oh, it would be a pleasure." She seemed amused.

I wasn't sure if she meant the research or the trouble would be a pleasure. Did I really want to get that close to a woman again?

Anyway, I kinda took the bait, after all. "Listen, it's lunchtime. You get a break? Can I buy you lunch?"

She looked pleased at the invitation but hesitated. "Oh, I, err...never eat lunch. I eat in the evenings. A soda, perhaps, or a tea?" She bustled about, phoning for someone to cover her desk. Although she turned away and covered the mouthpiece with her hand, I could still hear her side of the conversation. I heard her frustration growing. "Yes, I am going out for lunch today. I know. I know I never... But today I am going out. I need you to cover the section."

I strolled over to the foot of the stairs to give her some privacy. She was flushed and avoided my eyes when she joined me, fumbling with her handbag.

She didn't know the local diners well enough to recommend one, so I chose the nearest. We ordered and waited in an awkward silence until the sodas arrived. Then I made an attempt at conversation.

"Tell me, what does the initial stand for? Donna?" I hoped it would be.

"It is! How did you know?" She lit up with bright enthusiasm. I felt a warm glow, but it didn't last. It faded as she continued. "Have you been investigating me?" Her eyes twinkled mischievously. I ignored the hint. She continued, "Your work must be dangerous." She examined my eyes. "I do hope you are careful."

My heart sank. "How do you know what I do?" I tried to sound casual.

"Oh…" She stared down at her soda, failing to hide her guilty look. "I, well, I looked you up." She'd started slowly, uncertainly, then the rest came out in a rush. "I had your address from your library card and your phone number. I was curious about all these strange questions you keep asking, and so I looked you up in the phone book, and there you were. A private detective. How thrilling!"

Donna came to an abrupt halt, looked up at me, her eyes shining, then continued more slowly, stirred by her own words as she considered her soda again. "It was so exciting. The research. It was like being a detective myself." She lifted her head, and her eyes were gleaming again. "It must be like that for you every day, tracking people down and discovering facts and puzzling over them until you can see the whole picture. Such a feeling of fulfillment, of satisfaction!"

I fell into a dark place, a painful turmoil. She was drawn to me in a way I couldn't handle. I tried to deflate her enthusiasm. Just a little.

"Like a crossword?" I remembered she liked crosswords.

"Yes!" She grabbed my forearm, her eyes sparkling. "Like a crossword! Exactly!" She wasn't used to sarcasm.

Her passion spelled danger. A danger that thrilled me. A thrill I wanted to run from. Part of my brain saw Donna without those heavy-framed glasses, her hair hanging loose. It liked what it saw. Another part heard alarm bells ringing.

I wanted to push her away, to dampen her flame, to build a wall. "Except it's not like a crossword. It's about dirty secrets, and dirty lives, and angry lovers, and crooked cops. It's about following unpleasant people into dark parts of the city. It's about hearing lies from people who are afraid or who know too much. It's about telling the truth and breaking people's hearts and lying to keep them sane. It's about taking money from people whose lives are a wreck. It's not a game. It's not exciting. It's ugly. It's dirty. And I'm an investigator, not a detective."

She recoiled at my voice, at my words. They sobered her. She considered for a long time, stirring her soda with her straw. "Then why do you do it?" A quiet, disturbing question.

I had no answer for her. I had no answer for me.

15. MEMORIES

"Oh, Verity had such a time, back then, while you were at the war."

Mom had a clearer mind on my next visit. She was eager to talk. Her Verity couldn't be the same as mine. She just couldn't. But I had few other leads to follow, and I never turned down a free coincidence, even a hinky one like this.

Her eyes glazed over as her mind traveled in time.

"After your divorce and you came back to live with us, I know things weren't so good for you. Then you went off to war and your aunt Marion passed. I got awful lonely in that big, dark house. One day, Verity Jackson called by asking for you. You remember young Verity? She used to have quite a thing for you."

Damn! She *was* the same Verity. But were her memories all mixed up?

"Anyways, I told her you'd volunteered and wouldn't be around for a while. She was so disappointed. But such a sweet girl. Started coming 'round and keeping me company. I loved having her visit. Cheered me up no end with her tales. She had this sadness about her, though. She talked. Oh, how she talked. She knew all kinds of wonderful folk, important folk, movie stars and rich people, and all of them."

It felt good to hear Mom's voice and memory strong again—if these were real memories.

"And some of the things she got up to! Oh, my!" Mom giggled like a young girl, a look of amused guilt on her face. "But I shouldn't be telling you all this." Her pale skin actually managed to raise a blush. She crooked a finger, inviting me closer to whisper in my ear. "She even went with one big shot to that fancy place called the Mansion."

I took a breath before asking, "The Mansion?"

"Yes. Hearst Mansion."

"Castle? You mean Hearst Castle?"

"Yes. Castle. Ranch. That place." She waved her hand dismissively.

I felt the tension ease out of my muscles.

"That actor...dark hair and a wicked smile. You know the one!" Mom groped for the name then gave up. "He took her up the coast to the Hearst place one weekend. You know, they had such parties up there? And she met someone there who took her to that casino place." She stabbed a crooked finger at me. "Now, *that* was called the Mansion."

I really should've been prepared. I wasn't. It hit me in the chest like a stray bullet.

Mom continued to reminisce to herself, gazing into the distance, a sadness creeping into her voice.

"So she told me all her stories like I was her best friend. Seems she didn't have any real friends, just this Viola girl. Oh, they seemed to be so close, like sisters or something. Anyways, Verity dropped everything and went running to that man whenever he called, like some faithful puppy. I scolded her, but she wouldn't listen. I knew it would all end bad. Then she grew awful quiet, just sat gazing out the window and asking for news of you. Lots of silences when she visited. She had some great problem she wouldn't share with me. Ended up going to live with him permanent at his place up north. Didn't see her after that. Then I heard about the fire. Can't remember who told me…" She sighed the deepest and saddest of sighs I'd ever heard.

Her eyelids drooped. "So long ago. I'm pretty sure it happened like that, but so long ago…"

It was only a few years ago. But it all sounded familiar. I'd heard the same story from Isabella about her sister. And the Mansion was involved again. I didn't like this one bit.

Mom tugged at my sleeve. "But you've seen Verity, I know. That's her perfume on you every time you visit. And she was here with you when you visited before."

Ice ran down my back. I didn't know what to say. No easy and comforting lie came to my lips this time.

Her face crumpled as she waited for me to speak. "Oh, I forgot. It can't be her. She died, you know?" I spotted the sparkling of tears in her eyes before her head bent low and she began to sob. "She died. In that fire. Up north. It was terrible."

I pulled my chair closer to hers and drew her head down to my shoulder. I'd heard enough about Verity. It was upsetting Mom. I stroked her silvering hair slowly, gently, murmuring in her ear, reminiscing the way I thought she liked. Old stories. Happier times. Taking her mind off the hurt.

"Remember when we came to live on the coast, Mom? I was just a little kid. It was such a big adventure. You drove all those desert roads in the old truck, kicking up a dust storm behind us. I turned around in my seat and watched them out the back window till I fell asleep. I was so excited."

I didn't know if she was listening, but I kept going. "It felt like we drove for days. You headed into the sunset until we reached the ocean. And then you looked for Aunt Marion's address in the Bayville phone book, remember? But she wasn't listed. So we slept in the car all weekend outside the office she worked at. Early Monday morning, the sheriff pulled us in for vagrancy." I had to smile at the memory. "I was so scared of the cops. Then they phoned aunt Marion's office, and she came down and sorted it all out. Remember, Mom? Everyone laughing and happy? Remember?"

There was no reply. Her breathing was steady; her shoulders rose and fell slightly in a calm rhythm. I pulled myself out of the memories and looked at her face. She'd dozed off. But those memories still pressed at me. I heard my voice continue the tale that used to bring embarrassed chuckles in our home. "And the deputy at the desk took a shine to you. Deputy Jackson. A widower with a young kid. He's Bayville Sheriff, now." At last, my voice trailed off. I didn't want to remember the years that followed. Not my failed marriage, not the war…

I stayed that way, holding Mom in my arms, stroking her hair, lost in my private and far distant memories. Some time later, the nurse came to put her to bed.

————

My night was filled with confusion and terror, with fog and ghostly voices in the dark.

A blonde in a white gown floated through a dark castle dungeon. A spotlight hit the corner of the room, where a smiling Jimmy offered me a tumbler of my brand. I heard female screams echoing in the distance. Nearby, a low voice moaned and murmured in Spanish. Harry was there, rising from his wheelchair and smiling. From far away came the rumble of thunder.

No, not thunder: the pounding of heavy artillery.

The sound faded into the distance. The castle slipped away. Now there was a dark and silent forest, wreathed in a ghostly fog drifting through the trees. There were others moving in the murk all around me—my platoon—stepping forward in slow motion. My rifle was heavy in my arms, like a sleeping baby, ready to erupt with noise and violence. I murmured to it like I murmured to Mom, low and comforting. I spoke to it, shushed it, calmed it, calmed myself…

Too late! Everywhere the whoosh and roar of flamethrowers. Men screaming, running, erupting in flames. The acrid smell of chemicals and burning flesh.

And the screams! My God, those screams.

Rapid bursts of gunfire. The sleeping weapon in my arms jerking and exploding again and again.

And more screams—Rico!

Dear God. Rico. Right beside me, burning and screaming.

Someone, something, punching me in the chest and now it's *me* screaming in pain.

I jerked upright in the bed, still half-asleep, arms flailing, fighting someone grasping at me. Friend or foe? Made no difference. I just wanted it away from me.

I snapped fully awake.

Nothing there. No one. My whole body shook.

I checked again. I was alone. In my own bed.

Just another damn nightmare.

The castle, just a twist on the usual theme: my brain tricking me, lulling me until the forest ambush and the bullet ripping through my chest. Unless it's the other one, with me crawling through the forest mud on my hands and knees screaming from the pain in my chest and German Shepherds yapping and snarling in the dark all around me, hunting me, and my weapon gone. And then my unit swarming in and rescuing me.

Only my unit never arrives in the dream.

Slowly, the blood stopped pumping in my ears. My breathing eased. I felt the sweat cooling on my skin. Just a nightmare, I told myself. Just another nightmare. I struggled to push away the horrors into the back of my brain and flicked on the lamp to check the time. It was early, the small hours still. I had so many options. I could start my day and just grab a bottle and my smokes. I could try going back to sleep, praying I wouldn't return to those dark places.

I never made the choice. I froze. There was something in the room. A perfume scent.

That scent.

There was too much haunting me.

"Damnation!"

I forced my mind onto another path. Mom's talk of Verity's nightclub times had shaken me badly—if they were accurate. Hallucination? I didn't want to think about that again.

But movie stars? Verity as a good-time girl? That sweet, innocent kid I used to ignore back in Bayville? And my mom, laughing along with it all? My sweet, prim, silver-haired mother? My mom. Do we ever really know anyone properly? How had Mom really heard about the Mansion?

No. Her story was a patchwork of scenes from movies, scenes she'd put together to make up for the loneliness. Maybe she was already in decline before the blood clot downed her? But if it was made up, how had Mom really heard about the Mansion?

Still…I couldn't shake off the stuff about Verity and the Mansion or the way her story matched Isabella's about her sister.

Something came clear, and it hit me right between the eyes.

It wasn't a castle dungeon in the dream. It was the Mansion.

The scent slowly faded away.

16. ANOTHER INVITATION

Wednesday again. Did I mention I hate Wednesdays?

Another bad day. The guy with the inheritance problem phoned. He wanted me to tail his father's lawyer, to get some dirt on him to pressure him over the terms of the will. This time, I did tell him to go see a shrink. He got angry, shouting, ranting. I told him to go to hell and hung up.

Late afternoon. I was in a worse mood. Apart from the crazy guy, I had ahead of me an evening's tailing assignment. I hate tailing wayward husbands. I hate tailing.

So I was swiveling around in my chair, trying not to think about the visit to Mom or the evening ahead, just watching the day grow dark.

Through the open outer door, I spotted two shapes heading along the hallway toward me. This didn't look much like a social call. They were in suits this time, not tuxes, but I recognized the heavy one, Martino, from the Mansion. He needed a nickname.

I showed friendly, my way. "Hello, Marty and Nameless. Welcome to my place of work. Not as ritzy as yours, I must admit…"

They ignored my wise-guy routine. Nameless closed the office door and leaned back against it. Kind of him to make sure we were undisturbed. Marty ambled right in and towered over my desk, trying for silent menace. He needed to work on it some more. The scent of halitosis hit me.

"Make yourselves at home, boys. As you see, I'm between appointments."

Nameless was somehow the more threatening. Skinny, sharply dressed, slicked-back black hair, weasel-faced. He'd stood aside and let his bulky colleague show the muscle. I'd seen the Nameless type before. Quiet, examining his fingernails like nothing special was happening, playing sidekick. I knew who was in charge here. The quiet ones were the ones to watch.

Marty's ham of a hand reached inside his jacket. Could I reach my own automatic in the side drawer in time? I decided I couldn't. I waited, tried to look relaxed. His hand came out empty. He treated me to a mocking laugh. It wasn't a pleasant treat. "You got another invite to the Mansion, *Mr. Lake*. Mr. Caldera wants to meet you. Grab your hat, leave the gat. And we pat you down."

I chuckled and looked at Nameless. "Hat, gat, pat. Marty's a poet."

No reaction.

"Sure, pat me down, boys. Just don't enjoy it too much."

Marty's glare said we were never gonna be friends. The frisk was thorough. The bad breath came as a bonus.

"Should I grab my tux, boys?"

Nameless sneered at me. "Nah. It's informal. You got a back-stage pass."

I didn't know if it was good news or bad. I suspected bad, but it sure beat tailing a pathetic straying spouse.

————

The Mansion's gate guards waved us through. The parking area was empty. Too early for the rich folk to crawl out from their four-posters in their Hills homes. We pulled in at the rear door.

Marty jerked a thumb toward the building. I'd been through the service door before, at the previous manager's request. I accepted the polite invitation to climb out. They led me inside and down a long, narrow hallway to the end door on the right. I knew the way but didn't let on.

Nameless knocked.

We waited.

A small lamp above the door lit up. Marty opened the door and jerked his thumb again. His thumb was good with words. The goons didn't follow me in.

The room was gloomy. No windows. Dark wallpaper, dark furniture, dark mood. Except for the chandelier that looked like a little sister to the ones in the casino.

There was just one guy in the room. I guessed this was Caldera, manager of the Mansion for the Reno Mob, if I'd heard right. Expensive tailored suit, silk tie, shiny shoes. Tinted glass lenses. One of those hairpiece things that were always too dark for the age of the guy wearing it. Age? Maybe sixty.

A friendly, deep voice greeted me. "Welcome, my boy. Welcome to my home." He rounded the great mahogany desk, holding out both hands to wrap around mine. A strong, warm, dry grip—a boss's grip, a confident grip. "It's not often I get to play host to a war hero."

He moved to a well-stocked drinks cabinet. "Do take a seat. Your usual?" He held up a bottle of my brand. I nodded and eased myself down into one of the two overstuffed leather armchairs facing his ornate desk.

I looked around the room while he poured. Quality office furniture and a set of heavy drapes covering most of one wall. Looked like they hid a window, but it wasn't an outside wall. Who'd have a window inside a building? I figured the casino lay beyond the window, remembering the big mirrors on its walls.

The landscape paintings dotted around the walls didn't appeal to me, so they were probably high quality and high ticket. The small, framed photograph hanging near the door was out of place. It was the last thing he'd see as he left the room. Too small to make out from here, but I'd be walking past it on my way out. At least, I hoped I'd be walking out and it wouldn't be the last thing I'd see.

Some of the dates in his desk diary were marked with scribbles I couldn't read upside down at this distance. But I made out a big letter R circled in red for September 20th.

Caldera moved nimbly across the room and leaned over to hand me the glass. His smile seemed almost genuine.

He eased himself down into his leather desk chair and considered me for a while without speaking. He picked up the brandy balloon glass that sat waiting at his elbow. I considered him for a while, also waiting. This would be interesting.

Caldera continued savoring his brandy, swirling it and inhaling the fumes.

I got tired of waiting. "I think we both know why I'm here?" I bluffed.

His eyebrows brushed the ceiling. "We do, do we? I'm not so sure."

"Then you tell me."

"First, tell me about yourself, son."

"Nothing to tell."

"Oh, but you're a war hero. Third army and all. A volunteer, as well. Too old to be conscripted, I know." He looked sympathetic.

"Not a hero. I was there."

"Modesty is not a virtue I admire. Decorated, despite those various disciplinary issues."

"I don't like being told what to do."

He laughed. "I can tell. But you do understand I know all about you?"

I waited. He was just another someone dying to tell me a story. He'd get there when he was ready. He wasn't ready yet. Except to goad me. "Volunteered. I wonder what drove you from your mother's arms." Again, his heavy chuckle, before he turned serious again, playing Mister Sincerity. "I genuinely wish I could have been out there with you boys. Did my bit, though. War Bonds, fundraisers…"

Caldera saw he wasn't impressing me. He changed the subject. "When you visited the other night—and I do hope you enjoyed your visit—someone pointed you out to me. I recognized your name."

"Lake?" It came out as a snort.

"No, your real one."

"And?"

"I knew your mother, my boy. While you were away. We were very close. For a while." Beneath the blandness of his smile hovered something cruel. "Very close. She never mentioned me?" His expression showed a disappointment that slid into regret. "And now it's too late, I suppose, for her to tell you very much?"

I didn't give him the satisfaction of a response.

He continued, casual, conversational, bland. "Who do you think pays her trust fund?"

That floored me.

"How is she, by the way? For obvious reasons, I can't drop in on her. You do understand? I don't want to draw attention. I don't get out much."

Somehow, I found words. "Declining. You know how it goes with strokes?"

He nodded, making a show of sympathy. "Yes, I do. It is truly so heartbreaking. Such a vibrant woman to be so afflicted. When I heard about her illness, I set up a small fund to cover her care. I hope you don't mind? I can afford it. It seemed a small token of appreciation, after everything…"

I really didn't like this jerk's insinuations. I didn't like them one bit.

He got no response. He shrugged. "It seemed the least I could do for a dear, dear friend. You know, I'd rather hoped we could be friends, you and me. But you don't like me, I can tell." He waited. "I do hope that changes." His tone grew darker. "I honestly do." It sounded like a threat.

"After all, my name is about volcano fire and yours is about water. You'd get all steamed up if you try to play my nemesis." He chuckled to himself. "But I hear you have a temper already." He gave me time to simmer then added, "You *will* keep that crusading passion under control, won't you?"

Damnation, how I wanted to bust his face open right then.

"But right now, son, I want to give you a tour of my kingdom."

The sudden change of subject threw me again.

17. BACKSTAGE PASS

"Tour?"

"Yes, a tour of the *less public* areas." He crossed to the door as he spoke and opened it before I could reply. His two hoods stood waiting in the hallway.

"Come."

Looked like I had no choice.

Given the security, I wondered how any part of the building could be considered "public" at all. I'd heard stories, had a good idea what lay under the glitzy casino. I threw back the dregs of my Scotch and surrendered to the situation.

I grabbed a quick look at the photo as I exited. The corner of a log cabin overlooking a stretch of water. A rowboat tied up to a jetty. Handwriting scrawled across the bottom, "Bella Vista Cabin, Tahoe."

Just one more feature caught my eye briefly, then we were out into the hallway.

On the jetty stood a slim blonde dressed in white. Lousy photo. Couldn't make out her face.

He led me down a set of stairs to a hallway like the one we'd just left but with more doors. He was talking, playing tour guide.

"Not everyone gets to see what else the Mansion has to offer, only our most valued clientele."

And me.

"We'll skip the lower basement factory and the storerooms as well as the accommodation floors upstairs. I guess you've seen similar places before. But I think this might interest you. Some of our more energetic entertainment." He opened the first door.

A burst of female conversation and scents flooded out. A half-dozen girls were dressing for the evening. Not in the waitress outfits but the uniforms of private vice.

I was dazzled by the display of exposed flesh, narrow-waisted corsets, garters, exotic costumes…and silk masks like the one Maria had given me.

A couple of the girls showed interest, looking me over like they were shopping for meat. I'd seen that look before. Versions of Lyra.

Others were more subdued, as if passively waiting for attention. The other type of candy on offer, I guessed.

"Relax, girls. He's just a visitor. A tourist, not even window shopping. He won't be staying. And he *won't* be returning."

"Aww…" A girl in a skimpy leather outfit showed mock disappointment. She looked real hungry and licked her lips.

I was glad when he closed the door and headed off down the hallway, talking over his shoulder to me. "Speaking of girls, I do hope your friend, Miss Delgado, is not straying from her function here. Not getting wrapped up in curiosity. Curiosity *does* kill the cat, you know? She's such a pretty kitty and in such great demand. It would be such a shame for her and such a financial loss to me if she lost her attractiveness." He smiled. It almost seemed genuine. "But it happens to every woman, eventually, yes?"

He opened another door. I saw some of the furniture and held my ground. Someone, probably Marty, gave me a hard shove. I stepped inside. Dark crimson drapes hung across the naked stonework of the walls. No floor coverings, just cold stone slabs. A huge mirror on the wall. I guessed it was a one-way outfit like the one in the office. There was nothing else to see. Nothing except the furniture.

It was how I imagined an SS interrogation room would look. A bench, a throne-like chair, a whatever-it-was fixed to the wall. A rack of whips and things I never want to see again. Dead centre in the chamber was a crucifix tilted on its side so it looked like a great X, fitted with what had to be wrist and ankle straps…

He stood alongside the cross, smiling as if from fond memories, running his fingers gently, lovingly, along the wooden surface. "Oh, the fun we have had here." He looked me right in the eye. "Me and some of the people you know."

I wanted to rip his throat out.

"Before you depart—forever—I'd like to give you a going-away gift."

That didn't sound good. Not a ride into the desert, I hoped.

"A token of friendship to help you over this rough patch. You know, not having any current cases to pursue anymore." His emphasis was heavy, his meaning unmistakable. He nodded to Marty, who couldn't resist a glimmer of a grin as his hand slipped inside his jacket once more. This time it came out gripping an envelope. He offered it to me. I could guess what it contained. It felt like my birthday, the way all these envelopes kept coming my way.

"We won't meet again, *Mr. Lake*. You will look for some new clients. The trust will continue making payments. For now. And do stay away from my staff. I'd hate to lose Miss Delgado's rather excellent and popular services. Valuable, too." He really wanted to make sure I understood the alternatives. I held back the rising bile that burned like anger. This man loved having power over people and hurting them. I didn't want him to see how bad he was tearing me up.

My host waited. He'd had his say. Marty and Nameless stood behind me. Once more, it would be real impolite to refuse. Mostly, I didn't want to let loose with one of my rages, not with two armed goons behind me. I took hold of the envelope, weighed it in my hand, and considered it. Still he waited, his eyes boring into me through the tints. I grew more aware of the gorillas at my back as I delayed. The boss man stayed calm, confident.

I pocketed the gift and gave a tight grin. "Sure. Will do. So this is goodbye? I won't see you again?" I made it sound neutral. I didn't offer my hand. I knew we would meet again.

"Son, you really don't want to see any of us again. We'll drop you off in town. Then go invisible to me."

———

I wasn't going to let it go.

I didn't like being treated like a beat cop happy to turn a blind eye for a few bucks. Except it wasn't a few bucks. Another pile of Benjamins joined the collection in my safe—the air vent behind my sofa. Forget about it, IRS.

No, I wasn't going to let it go. But I had to take care, for Mom's sake, for Maria's sake. The Mansion was the center of a lot of bad stuff, worse than just its chemical factory and its dungeons. It was bad stuff that was too close to me.

But I didn't like taking orders.

I ran through the list.

A dead girl, Verity, and a dead friend, Harry.

Caldera, a mobster ruling his little kingdom under the snow-filled noses of movietown's rich and famous, claiming to be close to Mom and paying for her care.

Isabella's missing sister.

Sheriff Jackson's "hands off" warning.

The FBI playing footsie.

The Mansion's payoff and threats against Maria if I didn't back off.

Back off what? I still had no idea what I had so far.

And Verity's ghost...Verity Jackson? Really?

Too much bad stuff too close to me and too tangled up.

That photo of the cabin at Tahoe.

Lyra'd asked if I'd been to Tahoe yet. Mom said Verity had gone to a cabin "up north" with a guy from the Mansion. How the hell did Mom's Verity fit into the picture?

And there was that ghost…

―――――

Back at the library next day, Donna was helpful as ever. She found me a PI office in Reno, run by a couple of guys called Myers.

I spoke with brother Jake. Turned out he was an ex-marine. He sounded solid. He listened hard while I told him I was looking for some background on the place in the photo, Bella Vista Cabin at Lake Tahoe. I asked for its location, owner, whatever else sounded interesting. He knew what I meant. I liked the guy.

"Sure. It'll take a few days, though. The lake sprawls across two states and five counties, so I might have to visit a few land registries. I can get started tomorrow if there's no rush?" I told him it was fine. We agreed on a fee, and I left him to it.

The phone rang as soon as I hung up. I thought it might be Lyra. I hadn't heard from her in a few days.

It wasn't her. The wife of the straying bowling husband wanted to hear the worst. I'd forgotten about her. I gave some story about a head cold and offered to tail the man next week instead. She wasn't happy about it. Neither was I.

Friday, a guy phoned from some New Mexico hicksville called Roswell with some crazy story. Wanted to know if the motion picture people had been making space movies out in the desert back in forty-seven. If not, then maybe… He gave me his own version, something about crashed alien spaceships. I said I'd ask around and forgot about him.

A sweet couple from Kansas came by, full of grief and fear.

They sat wrapped in pain and confusion as they told me their story. Their sweet daughter, Catherine, had come to the big city, hoping to break into the movies. They had photos of her, lots of photos. They all showed a pretty girl, dark hair, smoldering eyes. They hadn't wanted her to come, they told me. She'd written home about auditions and agents and hopes and promises.

Then she'd stopped writing. Their letters got returned unopened. They'd driven over to check all was well and found out what a real classy place East LA was. It almost drove them crazy.

No one knew her at the address they had for her. The LAPD wasn't interested. Too busy, too many missing girls in movietown. So her mom and pop wanted me to look for her. They were worried sick. So they'd come to me as the local East LA guy for help.

They'd read about Elizabeth Short's murder a few years back. "Black Dalia," the press called her. She'd been a nice kid on the downward path when I met her, back when. Just another soul lost to the bright lights and dark lives of movietown. But that's another story.

The mother broke down a few times. The father, an older man, comforted her. He didn't look well; the grayness of his skin was a warning. Two more people broken by dream-chasing. Three if you counted the daughter. I took the photos and opened a new file.

I put on my reassuring smile, but it felt strained. So many girls hitting the big city with high hopes. Some ended up as waitresses if they were lucky. A golden few made it onto the screen, swapping a one-time walk-on part for some horizontal auditioning. Even fewer got picked up for a bit-part contract. A handful made it real big.

The rest?

The smarter ones swallowed their pride and went home.

The more desperate ones ended up working the bars and the streets, still clinging to an elusive dream long after there was nothing left for the camera. I'd ask Maria and a few of the other working girls I knew. I wasn't hopeful.

Too many lost girls, too many bars.

I turned down an advance payment. Looked like the old man'd be needing all his cash for medical care soon. I promised to do what I could as I showed them out. The old man wrapped both his farmwork-calloused hands around mine and squeezed hard as he pumped them, sharing his desperation and gratitude. "Thank you, son. Thank you so much." In his mind, the job was already done and his daughter was on her way home.

If only.

18. I HAVE A NAME

Catherine's last known address was only a couple of blocks over, so I took a stroll armed with a recent photo. I got the same blank stares and helpful responses from everyone in her building.

"What name?"

"Hot *chica*!"

"Never seen her. Wish I had. Tell her to come visit!"

"You lookin' for *chica*? I got good one for you."

I tracked down the landlord who—surprise—had never heard of her. There was no building supervisor right then; they were between hirings.

The beat cop shook his head. "These girls all look the same after a while."

So I hit the local bars. I asked Maria. No dice.

I chased down my usual friendly contacts in the red-light district, girls with names like Holly Wood and Beverley Hills. No dice.

So I started flashing the photo at all the barkeeps called Joe and the pimps with the biggest stables. Guess what?

I called the agency she said she'd worked for. They had her real name in their files, but they'd never gotten her any work, hadn't seen her for weeks, no new address on file…

Another soul lost without a trace. I felt I'd failed her. I felt I'd failed her parents. I had nowhere else to go on that one. Started to sound familiar.

———

Jake Myers called from Reno. He'd found the cabin.

"It burned down three years ago, September 20th. It was big news at the time. The owner and his girlfriend were killed in the fire. It's still up there, in ruins. I took a swing by and had a look." He gave me the address.

Girlfriend? That could wait. "What was the owner's name?"

I heard the rustle of papers. "Here it is. Vittorio Firenze, resident of LA County. Is that your interest?"

"Possibly. Early days, Jake, early days." I didn't want him getting too involved. Didn't want anyone getting too involved. I thought about Harry. I remembered Caldera's threats. "Just out of interest, you have Firenze's address down here?"

It was a lawyer's office. I should have guessed. "Closed coffin?"

"With that burning? There wasn't much left of the bodies. It's usual in these cases. I can check if you want. Does it matter?"

"No, let it go." Fire seemed to follow me around. "Out of interest, who inherited?"

"You'd have to check the documents at the county clerk's office down there for full inheritance details, but the Registry says the land transferred to a Pietro Caldera. Address is Firenze's lawyer. You still there?"

"Yeah, sorry, Jake. Just thinking." So the guy who ran the Mansion inherited the land. Could be a relative? Different surnames, but Mob names re often fake. And Family was often family.

"Those names ring any bells up in Reno?"

"Word has it Firenze was syndicate. I picked up nothing about Caldera."

"Any photos? Obituary pages, maybe?"

"Nope. No available photos. A very private man, our Mr. Firenze. Maybe ask the local PD, but I wouldn't waste my time. The obituary was just a three-line write-up."

Something else I wanted—needed—to know. "Just for the file, what was the girlfriend's name?"

"Lemme check. I got a note of it here. Jackson, Verity Jackson. From a place called Bayville, California."

For a moment, I couldn't breathe. Mom said her Verity had died in a fire up north. "Verity Jackson? Any other information on her?"

"Nope. Just a resident girlfriend. You know the type."

I ignored the locker-room slur about Verity. I felt protective. "Who identified the bodies?"

"Nothing to identify, charred too bad. His staff testified that the owner and the girl were the only ones in the cabin, and they didn't walk out. I got their names if you want?" He pressed on without waiting for a reply. "Firenze's driver, one Georgio Martino, was the main witness. He had the best English. The others were Julio and Lucia Gomez, husband and wife, gardener and housekeeper. The Gomez's were probably illegals, as they vanished soon after. Maybe went home. Convenient. Just Martino, then."

That would be Marty, the heavy at the Mansion. The old boss exited, he went to work for the new boss. Practical people, these guys. "Thanks, Jake. Send me your bill. And maybe we can do some more work together sometime? Reno's gotten to be an interesting place recently."

"Sure thing. And we could use a contact down there."

I thought Jake had finished. But he added something. "Before you go… Not sure if it's relevant, but it looks like the Feds were sniffing around for the same information."

Again, he'd grabbed my attention. "Talk to me, Jake."

"I slipped the Land Registry clerk a few bucks to tell me anything else of interest. Seems a guy in a dark suit was asking around a while back. Tall, blond guy. She guessed he was a Fed from his questions, and as Firenze was Mob, the movie seems to play that way. Anyway, blond guy was likely either Federal or Mob. Blond hair sounds more like a Fed. That's all I got. Any help?"

A blond-haired Fed close to the Mansion management? Fitted my old friend, Dutch. "You got me thinking. Thanks again."

"You take care, now. Especially if it's Mob stuff."

Yeah, I was gonna take real good care. Like asking around a little quieter than the way I was doing. Maybe.

I dropped in at the LA County court and looked up Firenze's last will and testament. Sure enough, the Tahoe land was left to Caldera. Everything else went to Firenze's daughter, Viola.

Viola? Mom said that was the name of Verity's only friend. Firenze's daughter, eh?

So the cash went to family and the land went to *the* Family. The Tahoe real estate was probably Mob-owned in truth and passed around the made men as needed.

So where was I in the investigation? Things were dropping into place, but I still missed the overall picture.

I still didn't know what Lyra really wanted. The guy in the photo was surely Firenze, taken on a visit to the Mansion before they died. And now he was six feet under. Lyra's claim about wanting to recover something of hers was flim-flam, like I thought. So what in hell's name did she really want?

I took the puzzle to my favorite thinking place. I knew everything. Or I knew what everyone had told me.

I took my phone off the hook and carried a bottle and a tumbler to my armchair. I sat gazing out at the crummy buildings across the street that blocked my view of the other crummy buildings. I rearranged the jigsaw in every possible way. The street lights came on. I couldn't work out how to make all those pieces fit together to make sense. Finally, the bottle was empty, the ashtray was full, and I'd dozed off.

A faint, familiar perfume crept into my dreaming head. I woke. There was only stale tobacco smoke in the air.

My armchair wasn't the best place to think, after all. There was maybe a better place.

My car knew where I wanted to go. My new thinking place.

I drove west down the Santa Monica Freeway, turning north at the Pier, looking for a half-hidden turnoff on the ocean side, leading down to an empty parking lot and a bar that didn't exist. There was already a hint of fog like I was expected.

———

"Welcome back, sir." Jimmy seemed pleased, but not surprised, to see me. His smile struck me as the only genuine thing in this place—the only genuine thing I'd seen for the past couple of weeks. A full tumbler waited for me on the bar. I didn't question it. I just accepted the madness. I scooped up the drink as I passed, heading for the door to the boardwalk. It was crazy. But this whole case was crazy. A blonde who wasn't, an evasive Fed, heavy warnings from sheriffs and brothel-keepers, half a story told by an old lady who wasn't living in the same world as me… How did they all hang together?

So how much worse was it to hope for a ghost to tell me more? At least everything Verity prompted out of me—or everything I'd dreamed from her—turned out to be true. I'd live with that, whether she was a dream, a ghost, or what the shrink called my subconscious. Yeah, I could live with whatever she was.

I settled down in the chair. I didn't have to wait long. The fog rolled in thicker and the foghorn started up. Over to my right, the lighthouse came to life. I closed my eyes, found I was holding my breath. When I had to exhale and sucked in the sea air, it was laced with a familiar scent.

"Verity?" The word came out before I could realize how stupid I was being.

"Who did you expect?" Her voice came from behind me, as before. She was chuckling. It wasn't mocking.

I didn't turn around. "Can I see you?"

Silence. I thought I'd lost her again. Then I heard soft footfalls, a board creaked, and she came into view. She took my breath away. Blond hair, hanging in delightful tumbles. A white gown, dressed for a swish event—or for the Mansion.

"Lyra?"

19. CONVERSATIONS

"Why did you think I was Lyra?" She chuckled, almost a giggle.

"Hair."

Verity nodded, smiling like she was pleased with me. "Why does a woman dye her hair?"

"To change her appearance."

"To look different from herself or to look like someone else? Do you think I look like her or she looks like me? Why do you think she wants to look different? And why at the Mansion?"

The questions spun around me. My brain worked through it. "So she looks like you. To draw the attention of someone who knew you? Someone at the Mansion?"

Verity smiled again, pleased with my progress. I liked that smile. I remembered how it looked on the young teenager. It looked better on a grown woman.

She was getting ahead of me. "Who might that someone be?"

Good question. Caldera was the best bet. I tried it.

"Aha! And now the big question. Why?"

I thought out loud. "He watches through the mirrors. He'd see Lyra and remember you."

"Why would that disturb Caldera? I was Firenze's girl. We died."

I snapped my fingers. "Damn it." I'd been blind. "Guilt! But he doesn't seem to be a guy who'd feel guilt. He just kills everyone in his way. Lyra was wrong. Her plan failed."

Her soft laugh sounded like tinkling bells. "Why should Lyra care?"

"Why the same perfume?"

"Don't you think Lyra might have shared hers with me?"

Okay, I could buy that.

"I think you are starting to believe I am the ghost of a dead woman."

I didn't know how to answer. This was crazy. I was talking to a ghost like it was normal, like she was a real person. But I didn't believe in ghosts, or I didn't.

I moved on. "So why does he hide from her? Why doesn't he just make her vanish?" She waited while I worked on it. "He doesn't need to. It's all about power. He enjoys watching her trying to bait him and failing. Sadistic bastard." That worked. "So why didn't she point me at Tahoe right off?"

She chuckled. "Maybe she likes her men to work hard to please her and to suffer along the way, to earn her approval?"

That fit. Also, my stumbling around in the dark would attract attention, reminding him that Lyra was still trying to get to him. It was an insane way to go, but I already knew Lyra wasn't a high-wire walker. More like a spinning top that's holding up for now but was gonna fall over with a crash sometime. I just hoped I wasn't around when she crashed.

I had another question. "So who pays the trust fund? Caldera?"

"Does generosity fit the man?"

"No. But he knew all about it and used it as a threat." I couldn't think of anyone else with heavy readies—and ready heavies—who cared about Mom. "Maybe his boys turned up the information about the trust?"

"He knew a lot about you. Name, war record, mother's trust fund."

How did Verity know about my talk with Caldera?

"Is he the only one who would remember me?" Verity asked.

"Maybe his henchmen? Marty was Firenze's driver." That took me nowhere yet.

"There's so much information available if you know where to look. You do lots of research yourself with sweet Donna." She smiled again, a warm smile of approval. Like maybe she knew something I didn't. How did she know about Donna? Hell, she knew a lot I hadn't worked out yet. Maybe Donna was something else I hadn't worked out yet.

I let it pass. Maybe I shouldn't have. Too late now.

She was still talking. "Why would Caldera pay the fund? Did he truly know your mother?"

"Caldera told me right out he knew her. But can I believe him? Was he pulling my strings to show his power? Was pulling the funding just a threat? Bastard knows all about me. But I know he's pulling Flynn's strings and the Feds'. They could've briefed him."

Verity held her silence. I'd been trying to sort out the answers I'd been given when I should've been asking the right questions in the right order.

It was the middle of the night. I grew tired; things grew blurry. I must've dozed off in the boardwalk chair.

I woke mid-morning. In my own bed. I didn't remember driving home.

Last night, I'd spoken with a ghost who knew all the answers to all my questions but made me work it out for myself. Sure, I'd gotten some answers. But not from Verity.

She never gave answers, just asked the right questions in the right order.

Was she real? Or was she a dream?

———

Verity's prompting made me realize there was another woman I needed to see.

It'd been days since I bought Donna lunch. That hadn't been a good idea. But I needed her. Needed her skills, I mean.

Donna welcomed me at the library desk like I hadn't wrecked her dime novel detective dreams last time. Another warm smile from another woman. But this woman was real.

Lyra and the women who came before, none of them was what she seemed. But Donna was just Donna. It was refreshing.

She tipped her head a little. Her brown eyes twinkled. "It's so good to see you again. You look like you need me for something. Well, I'm all yours."

Did she mean what I wanted her to mean?

She gestured around the archives level. "Another quiet day down here. No other demands on my time."

It was just me and her. I gotten what she'd meant. Or did I?

"Yeah, I need you. I mean, I need you to look something up for me."

Her expression changed a little. "You know, I should start charging commission. Or become your partner."

I thought I'd killed her girlish fantasy about my work. I ducked the issue. "Dancing partner? Sure, I'll take you dancing sometime." I ended with a grin.

Her eyes told me she'd gotten the joke, but she followed through. She was too smart for me. "Oh, I'd love to go dancing with you." She glowed.

Damn it, I was digging a deeper hole every time I spoke. I changed tack. "Meanwhile, can you find out who owns a place called the Mansion, out in the sticks? And whose name is on the liquor license?" There was no street address. I gave her the nearest town as a pointer.

She said she'd find out for when we met again. Something told me she wanted to keep me coming back. After all, she wasn't rushed off her feet right now.

Donna filled me in on the stroke thing I'd asked about. Seemed like she didn't realize it was personal. She told me straight. I'd already heard this stuff. It was as depressing as when the doctor said it. Incurable. Decline of memory and thinking over time. Possible anger outbursts. Possible detachment from reality… It all fit.

So Mom's Verity could be just a fantasy. The name just a coincidence. I'd play it that way until I learned different. I wanted it to be just wishful thinking. It was better for me. If Mom's Verity was a fantasy…what was *my* Verity? Was all of Jimmy's my own fantasy? Maybe I should get checked up by a medic. Sure, next week, next month, sometime.

As I drove away, I thought about the cute, mousy, helpful librarian I'd met just a week or so ago. Donna was in my life now and wanted to be in deeper. Less of a mouse these days. Or was I misreading her totally?

Men were easier to understand. There was a guy I could pump for information.

I knew where to find Sgt. Flynn evenings. The Pride of Ireland bar, down near the beach front. I waited till late. I wanted him loosened up at the cost of the bar owner who was paying his dues to LAPD's finest to be left alone.

"Hello, Finflynn. Let me buy you one." I plopped down on the bar stool next to his, grinning my best grin.

"Whaddya want?"

"Hey, don't growl at me. I just offered you a drink." I nodded to the barman and pointed at the empty tumbler in front of the cuddly cop.

"You eejit. You got a pile of chutzpah. You come for favors like I'm your oldest, bestest friend."

The refilled glass slid into his line of sight. He thought about it. He shrugged. He grabbed it. "All right, whaddya want? Make it quick, then vanish."

"Just a question. About Bayville."

He scowled at me. He remembered. He said nothing.

"Sheriff's right-hand man, yes?"

He nodded. "Damn right, I was." He took a slug of Irish.

"You knew him well."

Again, a bleary nod. "Like twins in a pea pod."

"What happened to his daughter, Verity?"

I never saw a man change so fast. He swayed to his feet and grabbed at my throat. I tried to dodge, but he held my collar in a mighty fist. "No! That fire killed her and broke his heart. Nearly died of grief. The other filthy stuff had turned him white before that. He wants it all buried. And I told you not to be asking around about it. It'll break the old man. I swear to God, I'll rip your throat out."

"Okay, okay." I raised my hands, palms out like I was pushing him back without touching. "My mistake."

The outburst drew attention, and I guessed the local boyos would all be on his side. But now he looked nervous, maybe realizing what he'd blurted out. He leaned closer to hiss into my ear. His breath stank of booze. "I'll do you one favor and not tell him you wuz asking. Only cuz I don't wanna upset him. But if ever you run up against me again... Now disappear." He released me as the boys gathered around. I eased a path through them, real polite, and disappeared out the door.

Sure, I could have driven up to Bayville and asked around, but Flynn told me more than I'd get from hours talking with the good townsfolk. Much more.

I thought I had it all worked out. Time to talk with someone else.

At home, I sat down with a bottle, a glass, my smokes, and the phone book. There were only a few Firenzes listed. I didn't bother looking for a Lyra or even a Viola. Names seemed flexible features for her. I just started at the top and worked my way down. I asked a few stupid questions to anyone who replied and went back to dialing. None sounded like Lyra. Then—third time lucky—I hit paydirt. The moment I heard that bored and sultry voice, I knew it was her. Once more, I apologized, claiming a wrong number, and noted the address. Interestingly, she was listed under her real name.

Time to meet the lady in her lair. The lady of the lake.

20. LYRA'S LAIR

The apartment house was pretty swanky, near the Hills where the stars come out for pay but not snuggled down among them. I started to straighten my tie as I neared the secure plate-glass doorway. I changed my mind. What the hell.

The uniformed guard scowled at me from the comfort of the reception desk. Overweight. Retired cop. Standard-issue private guard. He dragged himself to his feet and ambled over, one hand on the butt of his police special. "Name, who do you want to see, and are you expected?" It was a script he'd memorized. Clever boy.

He didn't like being disturbed from the sports pages, I could tell. Also, I could tell he didn't like me. It was probably my cheap suit. And my crooked tie. He'd become a snob, working for the nobs.

I flashed my driver's license and gave Lyra's real name. "Viola Firenze." I said I was expected. Maybe I was. He looked dubious but strolled back to the desk and spoke briefly on the house phone. I saw him nodding, so I threw him a smirk.

He unlocked the doors and pointed at the elevator. "Top floor." He went back to his racing tips. His work was done. Good boy.

No name tags on the floor buttons. Visitors were supposed to know where they were headed. I straightened my tie again, checked my reflection in the full-length mirrors, and jerked it loose again.

The lift slid to a soft halt. A few doors led off the hallway. One stood ajar. My invitation. I paused at the door and called out, "Miss Firenze?"

"Come." She was using her boss-lady voice. She stood with her back to the door, facing out a French window overlooking the city. I wished I could afford a view. Any kind of a view.

But she was the view that held my eyes. Her black negligee hung down to her ankles. It must have been silk, the way it clung to her curves and was nicely see-through. There was nothing between fabric and flesh. Her hair hung loose. Bedroom elegance on heels. Yeah, she wore heels.

Lyra spoke without turning from the view. "I was expecting you."

That would explain the heels and negligee. She'd made an effort for me. Nice. "You recognized my voice on the phone."

She snorted. "Wrong number, indeed!"

When she'd let me have a long rear view, she turned, her face deadpan. The belt was tied loose. Her cleavage almost reached her navel. She eyed me up and down like I was a piece of meat as she took a sip from the wine glass in her hand.

I ignored her play, hung my hat over the back of an armchair, and dropped into it.

She threw me the superior, amused lip -pursing she did so well. She'd played her opening hand, and I'd played mine. Ground rules established. The game began.

"Drink?" She indicated a cabinet with her glass but made no move toward it. I wasn't gonna play fetch for her.

I took in her luxury living room. Expensive armchairs, tasteful throw rugs, dark wood furniture, the works.

A simple tapestry piece hung on the wall. A child's work set in an expensive frame. Wobbly letters spelled out, "In my Father's house there are many mansions [John 14:2]."

I nodded toward it. "Appropriate."

Again, I felt that Alaskan wind in her glare. It still didn't work on me.

Her negligee parted to the thigh as she strode on those long legs toward me, a predator closing on its prey. Her breasts swayed under the thin silk, deliciously teasing a sudden and dangerous reveal. Maybe it was contact with the fabric or maybe she was pleased to see me. I tried to keep my eyes on her face.

It was tough.

She lowered herself elegantly into the armchair facing me, just a few feet away. She crossed her legs. The silk parted. She let it hang. I still kept my eyes on her face. It was getting tougher. But I'd gotten her to move toward me. I was winning.

You'd never have guessed it from the way she spoke. Languid, I thought it was called. "So, Mr. Investigator. You finally worked out who I am. I usually expect my men to take their time. But not in this case."

"Yeah, about the case." I thought we'd never get there. Now she was so close, I caught a whiff of familiar perfume. Memories flashed—our first meeting in my office, Jimmy's bar, the Mansion casino, the lingering hint of scent when I woke from my nightmares.

I pulled back to the here and now. "About the case, Miss Firenze. You hired me to find a man. I found him. He's buried in a coffin near Tahoe. But you knew that."

She sipped at her wine again and gave a knowing look. She wanted more from me. Tough.

"I did what you asked." I stood. "So the case is closed. My expenses burned up the advance, so we're quits."

Her calm facade crumbled. She set down her wine and stood, glaring at me. The silk fell closed around her legs. She tugged at her belt to close the top. Offer withdrawn. Ah, well.

I pushed a little. "One thing I'm curious about. Why not tell me it was your father? I'd have had a name to start with."

"I wanted to see how good you were. Obviously, I was misinformed about your abilities. You may keep the payment. Please leave."

"Oh, I did okay. I found your father. I found Verity."

The name hit her hard. "And?"

"And nothing. You didn't pay me to find Verity. That was just conversation. No charge. And anyway, I think you just fired me." I grabbed my hat.

"Is that it?" Her voice was a whiplash. "Don't you want to know more?"

Sure, I wanted to know what she really wanted from me. "What else is there I would care about?" I half-turned toward the door.

"Verity's murder…"

Sounded like she cared more about the girl's murder than her own father's.

"Murder?" I threw her my best innocent look.

"I did not major in Law. I call it as I see it. I see murder."

"Okay, Lyra, I already got that much. It was some Reno Mob war. Caldera took out your father. Verity Jackson was an innocent bystander. You tried to make him feel guilty at the murders by turning up at the Mansion and used me to stir things up more. Did you really think it'd work? Well, it's failed. Go to the cops."

"You know I cannot do that." She kicked off her heels. Maybe she thought her seduction ploy was played-out.

"Yeah, the Feds are on Caldera's payroll, and Sheriff Jackson's ashamed of his daughter being a mobster's plaything. He's likely being blackmailed or getting a payoff to keep his peace. Tough. Welcome to movietown."

"There's more."

"What did I miss out?"

"Why I created your mother's trust fund." She'd seen an

opening and grabbed the ball back. Lyra was sliding back into her controlling self.

Seemed like everyone wanted to claim credit for being a trust fund angel. "So Daddy left you a stack of cash…" I looked around the apartment. "A big stack. You used some to set up the fund. I should thank you for that." But I didn't know *why* she'd done that or if payments would continue. I realized how thin the ice underfoot suddenly got.

"You can thank me later." She smirked. "Yes, I inherited rather a lot, and there was a hefty insurance. I used it to good purpose."

"Okay. Now tell me *why*."

Lyra—I still thought of her as Lyra—considered me. I guessed she was deciding her next play, whether to play boss-lady or come clean. She turned and made her way to the bureau. Her body moved with a natural elegance instead of her usual dominating stride. I kinda liked it. Maybe the games were over? She reached inside an ornate box on the bureau. I expected some great reveal—a document, a letter, a photograph…

She took out a pack of long cigarettes and shook one out as she gazed into the distance like she was seeing something I couldn't. Memories? She tapped the cigarette a few times on the back of her hand before slipping it between her lips. Even at a time like this, stressed and distracted, she stood waiting for some lapdog to bring fire.

Lyra'd started opening up, and I wanted more information. I negotiated with myself the terms of my surrender. I crossed to her and sparked my Zippo.

She held back her fake-blond hair and lowered her head to the flame, sucking in the first taste of smoke like some holy incense. She held it in, savoring it, before looking into my eyes without a trace of gratitude and exhaling slowly in my direction.

The whole performance set me alight. And I was standing so damn close I could smell her scent—*that* scent.

She held my gaze, her cold face back in place. She inhaled deeply again, straightening her back so her breasts lifted.

I watched. I waited.

Exhaling a long, smoke-filled sigh, Lyra picked up a fancy ceramic ashtray. She turned and made her way back to the French windows, her fingers stroking along each piece of furniture as she passed. She stood with one elbow resting on her free hand as she stared out into the night, past the lights, not at any object but at those far distant memories.

It felt like the right time to ask. "Verity belongs to the arm in the photo? And they visited the Mansion back then, before the Reno Mob took it over?"

She nodded. Still gazing at some distant place and time, she spoke quietly. "Verity hid at your mother's place when things got bad." She glanced over her shoulder. "You didn't know?"

So it was true. I didn't react. I needed to know *why*.

She turned back to the view she wasn't seeing. "Verity had no one to turn to when things got bad. She came looking for you, but you were off being a hero in Europe. Verity and your mother both needed you, and you were not there for either of them." She just had to add that little bite.

I took the bait. "Yeah. The war was a bundle of fun. But no pay phones in the barracks. Her letters didn't say how bad things were for her." I shut my mouth before I spilled too much guilt on the pricey flooring.

Lyra's sigh was heavy with sadness. "I was so grateful to your mother for helping to save Verity for a while. I was away in New York when it happened."

"Verity was your daddy's mistress, just a little younger than you. You were close? Like sisters?"

She snorted her contempt. "Verity was no sister. She was... special to me."

She stared down at her cigarette in silence, then looked up at me again. "For the rest, you were right. Caldera set the fire.

Killed them both." She stubbed out the half-finished cigarette slowly, grinding it into the ceramic like she was trying to destroy something there. "Reno had taken the Mansion away from Joey Milan's East Coast Mob about then. They sent Caldera to run it for them."

"And Marty? Martino, Caldera's muscle? He was your daddy's driver. Served two masters?"

She paused. "He's loyal to who pays him and the Family."

"Go on."

"I wanted Caldera to suffer for what he'd done. He has everyone in his pocket. Who could I turn to? So I dyed my hair and dressed like Verity and started turning up there." She laughed. A self-mocking laugh. "I hoped he would feel guilty. Perhaps it worked. I do not know. But I am sure he watches me through those mirror things." Her hand trembled as she reached for another cigarette but changed her mind and looked up at me instead. "And Verity's not the last girl he's killed that way—or the first."

"What way?"

She turned to face me. "Verity was different."

Pause. "She was special."

Longer pause. "To me."

Another long pause. "Very special."

Lyra laid down the smokes and the ashtray and crossed the room. She stood very close to me. Her arms hung at her sides. She looked up at me, her face full of pain. She had thrown away the boss-lady, the dominant ball-buster. She stood within reach, open and defeated and lost and vulnerable. "I loved her." She reached out for me.

Tears welled in her eyes, ran down her face, smeared her mascara. Her body trembled, wracked with a sobbing I couldn't bear to watch. I threw down my hat. I wrapped my arms around her. I hugged her close. She pressed her whole body against mine. She lifted her chin, her glistening eyes exploring my face, seeking something. Her lips parted. Her eyes begged me for comfort.

I melted. I comforted her.

Like I said, I was a sucker for a damsel in distress.

21. AFTERGLOW

I lay on my back next to her. She was turned away from me, her breathing slow and steady. Her head lay on my arm, pinning it. I didn't want to wake her. I wanted time to think.

She hadn't had a chance to draw the drapes, we'd hit the bed so fast.

Her bedroom was so different to Maria's. Bigger, with expensive furnishings and ornaments.

Daylight was starting to burn away the night. Out the window, the stars were fading. Tiny sparks lost to a greater light.

But I knew the darkness was still out there, hiding in the shadows. It always was. Damn! I was tired.

She'd stopped sobbing before we hit the bed. I'd been taken.

It had been a long night. A very interesting night.

My thoughts ran around in circles in the silence.

She murmured, her voice soft and relaxed. "You're thinking about Verity." She didn't turn around. "It is not polite to think about another woman while in bed with me. You need training." She couldn't resist being on top.

"You said you loved her?"

Lyra took a deep breath, and her words came wrapped in a slow, painful memory.

"Yes. I did. So very much."

"She's the thing that belongs to you, that was taken away."

"Yes."

"Did you share your perfume with her?" I held my breath, waiting for the reply. It would explain a lot.

She snapped over her shoulder at me. "Is this relevant?" She'd prepared her lines and wanted to stick to the script.

"Yes."

"Very well, yes, I did share my perfume with her. And much, much more."

"So you were lovers. But she was Daddy's mistress. Big obstacle? From what I know of you, I guess nothing stopped you. You started before he'd finished with her?"

Silence.

"So she was Daddy's toy and you loved her. Go on."

"I hated her." Cold, flat, emotionless. A statement of a fact she'd lived with for a long time.

"You said you loved her."

"I did. Loved her for what she was, hated her for being addy's plaything."

"And she belonged to you at the end."

"She did. Totally. But she had to pretend to Daddy." Lyra pulled free of my arms and stood. She threw me another curve ball. "She could have been yours, you know?"

My mind stumbled down a flight of stairs. "What?"

Her naked body moved like an invitation. She lit one of her long cigarettes and stared out the window, retreating into a shroud of silence marked by the wisps of smoke. I hadn't seen her face at all this morning.

"She loved you. That's why she went seeking you out when she got confused about me and Daddy. A place to hide. A guy she really loved."

"Hell, I knew her when she was a kid. She was too young. I was too young…"

Lyra didn't turn from the window. "She spoke of you and

Bayville. She had a crush on you. You crushed her in return. Made her dependent, looking for someone older who would pay her attention. She found Daddy. Then she found me, just a little older but…"

She sucked at the cigarette. "Mother died in childbirth. It would have been a brother. Daddy always wanted a boy. He raised me to be tough."

That explained a lot.

"I was only a few years older than Verity, but I was the right person for her, as you were not available."

I forced down the guilt. "So that's the real reason you brought me into this. To punish me. So I could make up for what I did to her over ten years ago? Christ! She was just a friend to me."

"A friend? Just a friend? That's all she was to you!" She ground the half-smoked cigarette into an ashtray. It looked like an anger habit.

I needed a change of subject. "Why not face Caldera when he's away from the Mansion?"

She lowered her head and shook it slowly. "He never leaves. Just to the airport sometimes, random dates, in a fast car filled with his thugs. Private plane. I cannot follow him. I assume he's meeting his Reno mobster friends."

"Yeah. Monthly meetings. Sounds right. He has a big R marked in his diary for the twentieth."

Lyra lifted her head. She nodded slightly and turned to face me. Smirking, she advanced slowly toward the bed. "You know, I gave you the runaround, but you got there in the end. I think you did all right."

"Just all right?"

She scowled a mock frown and lay down next to me. "Okay, I'm impressed." She took my face in her hands and looked deeply into my eyes. "Now impress me again."

"You'll have to wait till the scratches on my back heal." A good enough excuse to delay things.

"I can bring salt." She sounded optimistic.

"Remind me why you hired me. Apart from revenge."

She sighed wearily. "Always questions. I'll tell you, then we stop talking for a while." She took a deep breath. "Daddy's people knew about your mother. He yelled at me and told me Martino was following Verity. Martino would have told Caldera, who had his contacts research you. I thought if you started sniffing around clumsily, you'd draw attention, make things even more uncomfortable. And give me some leverage…"

"Thanks for your confidence in my abilities."

She shrugged, then pouted, and ran a fingertip along the scar tissue on my chest.

"So what happened after I started being clumsy?"

"Nothing. No reaction at all."

She was wrong. There'd been a reaction from thugs, and Feds, and cops.

"You wanted me bumbling around, stirring up the whole hornets' nest. Drawing attention to me and back to you. So I was just someone expendable in your revenge mission. And what do you want in the end?"

"I want Verity's life back." Sharp, bitter words.

"You can't have that, no matter how rich you are."

She turned into Alaska again. "He has the life of someone who belonged to me. He took her from me. He owes me. And you owe Verity. A life for a life." Alaska melted. Her fingers took a walk across my stomach. "You know, we could be together if you help me…"

I was getting her drift. Played again! I rolled away and sat up. "So this whole damn thing was to draw me in to be your revenge killer, not just to stir up Caldera? Well, it stirred up a hornets' nest, and they're swarming all over me. I'm done with you and your lies. I'm not one of your puppets. I'm not helping anyone commit murder."

"I can pay. And offer much more besides…" She did that one-eyebrow-raised thing.

"Miss Firenze, I don't think you're used to being on the back foot. Well, *I* don't like being made to dance on a string. I don't like wild goose chases and red herrings. I don't like being lied to."

"No more lies, I promise. Not anymore. Just do one thing for me, for Verity." Her eyes brimmed full.

I swung my legs off the bed and reached for my pants. "I reckon it's time to go."

She grabbed my shoulder. "Come back here!" It was an order. But then her voice turned distant. "You might be the last man I ever bed."

I shook her hand away. "Huh. No one compares? Go on, tell me another lie." I didn't look at her.

"No. It's not that." Her voice sounded real strange.

That made me look at her. She looked away, hiding her face. I was too late.

Something told me I shouldn't ask what she meant. As it turned out, maybe I should've.

Lyra didn't look my way again.

I dressed.

I left.

22. A DEATH

Late afternoon, Maria called. Her friend Isabella had more information. "Come to my place tonight. Not too late."

Lucky she couldn't see the resignation I felt creeping over me. I had another girl on my mind. But Maria was Maria. "Okay. After I close up for the day. I won't be too late."

"Okay, my Sir Lancelot. You are the best!"

At least she wasn't asking for another Mansion meeting. That would've been a problem after Caldera's threats.

It was dark when I parked up in the alley behind her block and strolled around the old building. I saw the flashing lights before I reached the corner. Red lights like flares hit the walls and slid down like runaway fire.

Red lights. Cops.

Two police cruisers, roof lights competing with cheap neon flashes from the bars across the street. A crowd of the curious—passers-by, neighbors, curiosity seekers, journalists... Two uniforms doing apathetic crowd control.

I flashed my ID at a bored cop. "Who's in charge?"

He nodded toward a bulky raincoat filled by my good friend Sgt. Flynn, a car radio handset pressed against his mouth. He was staring at me hard. Flynn waved me over, and the cop let me through. He ended his chatter as I got within earshot.

"Well, hello, boyo." He wore a cruel smile as he strolled toward me. "Don't tell me you have another coincidental visit to another friend who coincidentally just died?"

"Depends who just died." I held onto an unreasonable hope.

"Some Mexican whore." He sounded bored. I felt a cold chill.

He checked his notebook. "Third floor, Maria Delgado. Illegal." He glanced up at me. "A hobby horse you been riding?"

It was hard to speak. I managed somehow. "I know her."

"Knew her, you mean. Come on up. Tell me all about the little *puta*."

I'd said I wouldn't be too late. I'd failed her. I was too late.

A fog filled my brain as I followed his waddling bulk up the stairs to her room, barely hearing his wheezing narration. "Neighbors heard shouting. Nothing new there. She was noisy in bed, eh?" He paused, giving time for the taunt to sink in. "Then gunshots. That was new. A neighbor called it in from the bar across the way. Should I tell you it's not a pretty sight?" He glanced back at me. "Naw, I won't bother. Was she pretty?"

The patrolman guarding the door stumbled as he stepped aside. Young, pale, drained. He stank of vomit's acid-sweetness. He needed to change his uniform shirt.

Flynn burbled on. "Damn soft kids we're recruiting these days. Murder scene virgins. Threw up in the sink. Blocked it." The boy winced and brushed at the stains on his shirt. Flynn snarled at him. "Get out, kid. Send up a grown man to stand around in the hallway."

The officer threw me an embarrassed look and scooted.

The living area looked much as I'd last seen it. Nothing disturbed. Not a burglary gone wrong. But who would bring a gun to rob someone living in this lousy block, anyway? Everything was there: the frilly do-das around the place and on the dresser, the framed photo of the little girl and the old woman in front of the grocery store.

Except it wasn't there.

Flynn's voice cut through my thoughts. "She's through here." He stood at the open bedroom door. "Right where you'd expect a whore to be."

I swallowed my anger. Took a deep breath to prepare myself. Stepped forward and peered in.

Bedroom.

Bed.

Blood.

Body.

She was dressed. Somehow that made me feel a little better. As if dignity mattered anymore. Sprawled on her back, arms thrown wide like she'd fallen that way. Blood splatter across the wall, across the drapes, across the wooden crucifix on the wall. Blood-soaked bed covers. Blood-soaked body. Blood-soaked raven hair.

No face.

Just a red, pulpy mess.

"Point blank hit with a high caliber. Always messy. Blew away her face and the back of her head. You can see the bone splinters and gray stuff."

My stomach cramped, clenched. My throat burned with acid. I staggered for the bathroom.

Flynn didn't let up for a moment. He followed me across the room and leaned on the door frame, watching me splash water on my face. He kept talking like she was just meat. "Looks like nothing taken, not that she had anything worth taking—"

I was across the room, grabbing his throat, slamming him against the wall. My nose pressed against his, smelling his sweat, tasting his sour whiskey breath and his fear. Pop-eyed and terrified, he mouthed something I couldn't make out through his muffled gurgling.

"You bastard, Flynn. He took everything she had. Her *life*!"

I gripped his throat tighter. I gripped him for Maria. I

gripped him for my pain. He struggled with the strength of a man about to die. He was heading for hell, and he knew it.

A tap on my shoulder. A quiet voice, polite and calm. "Sir, please release the sergeant."

It took a long time for the words to sink in. Slowly, slowly, I relaxed my grip.

"You saw that!" the fat man gasped out, bent over, clutching his throat.

"Sorry, Sarge, I just saw you and the civilian talking quietly." This was the grown man Flynn had called for.

From somewhere far away, I heard Flynn's voice raging at the officer. "You'll pay for that, you gobshite!"

The fire of anger still rushed through me. I swayed, held onto the door frame. Heard thunder in my ears. My body stayed fired up for the fight, for the kill.

Flynn turned his anger back to me. "Get out! I won't forget this, you whore-fucking bastard!"

I took one last look at the bed, the body, the red mess, the missing face, the silver crucifix still dangling from her neck…

"Maria…" It came out as a sob. I was shaking. Thunder rumbled in my head.

The patrolman took my arm and guided me toward the door. "Go home, sir. Sgt. Flynn has your contact details, I think."

I forced myself to calm down, heard myself whisper, "Thanks, officer." I wasn't sure if I meant thanks for stopping me killing a cop or for the cover-up lie.

Flynn's throat still sounded raw. "I said get the hell outta here. You got bad attitude, boyo, and a temper that'll land you in the morgue. Too many of your friends started getting killed again. I'm watching you real close from now on. Like a hawk watching sheep. You hear me? Don't so much as jump a red light in this town for the next hundred years!" His hoarse yelling echoed down the stairwell behind me. "And don't leave town. This ain't over!"

Leave town? If the killer had taken the photo, he knew where

Maria's family lived in Mexico, and he intended going there. I had to warn them. Leave town? I'd be leaving the whole godforsaken country.

I was filled with too much to cope with. Maria gone? The scene in the bedroom, the wall, the red mess, the need to warn her family… Crazy how you thought of things to do, things to push back the pain. I was lost, a sleepwalker in a street full of flashing lights and pain and memories and—

Yes, I had to warn Maria's family. I had to warn them, phone them, or maybe I'd have to drive there.

The photo. I could see the photo in my mind. But the address, the phone number? Gone.

I'd seen those details a hundred times. But they were gone.

I couldn't warn Maria's grandma. She, too, would be gone.

No point asking the LAPD. They didn't care about some old woman in some nameless one-horse town somewhere in Mexico. I didn't even know if Grandma was still alive. Maria was an illegal, so no family contact details on file.

I couldn't ask at the Mansion. I didn't know how to find any of her friends. It was hopeless.

Someone in the crowd was calling my name. I started walking. He kept calling.

The someone grabbed my arm. I closed my eyes. I was still hopped up on anger. I still wanted to kill someone. Not Flynn, not this guy, but Maria's murderers. I knew it was the damn Mansion crowd. And it was my fault for not letting the case drop. I knew for sure it was because I'd ignored the threats. Hell, I'd even spent the night with Firenze's daughter.

I shook off the arm and turned, tensed and ready.

"Hey, card shark. It's me. Take it easy." It was Mike from the poker nights. Mike, the small-time journalist. Small-time, like everyone at that table—me, him, dead Harry, and the others. He stepped back, terrified, when he saw my face. "You okay?"

I thought about it, trying to calm down. I nodded. "Yeah. Okay." I lied.

"I saw you come out. Talk to me. What happened? Someone got shot? The cops are saying nothing. Talk to me. Client of yours?"

It boiled up and spilled over. "Just another cheap whore got her face blasted away. Someone's daughter, someone's grand-daughter. Nothing new, nothing for your front page. No Pulitzer for you here." I turned to go.

"Hey, man, you look like crap. Listen, you need a drink. C'mon. My treat."

I hesitated.

"Look, no questions." He slipped the notebook into his jacket pocket. "Just a couple of dogfaces who lose too much at poker together. Ex-GIs having a drink together, okay?"

I didn't remember much more. Nothing much happened to remember. He took my arm and guided me to the bar, ordered and paid, witnessed my angry silence for…I didn't know how long. And not a single question. Mike's a good guy. He'd left the murder scene, lost the story. He'd asked me no questions. That's why he'd always be a second-rate reporter. And that's why he'd always be a good guy. We needed more good guys.

Oh, yeah. Some bar girl came over with a wide grin and hungry eyes. I told her I wasn't interested. She said my eyes had been on her all night. She was wrong. My eyes were on her silver crucifix. Something about that crucifix… My mind was foggy.

It reminded me of Maria. But somehow it didn't. I was tired. I was in shock. I'd had too much of the day and too much of the booze. Time to go. Mike staggered out with me and said to call whenever I wanted. Good guy, Mike.

I looked around the street. The air was cooling fast. The street was quiet, empty. The cops had gone; the crowd had gone. Yesterday's news. It must have been near midnight. I remembered I had something to do…

Yeah, I had to phone the Mercado Delgado. But I had no address, no number.

"*Buena suerte*," I whispered to Maria and to an old woman far away over the border. "Goodnight." It was all I could do.

It was another day I wished I'd never seen.

I dreamed about a laughing, sexy, clever, vibrant Mexican girl who loved life and what she could claw from it. A girl who'd never known her parents. A girl who'd been brought up over a run-down store in a run-down town by her grandmother. The girl in the photo. The girl who still wore her rough-carved wooden crucifix no matter how expensive she was dressed. She only took it off when she was in bed with someone. Maybe to hide her guilt… Yeah, she could feel guilt. She was Catholic. Guilt sustained Catholics. I knew all about that.

Maria, a girl who…

There it was again. Some thought slipping in and out of my mind, my dreams…

I hoped for my muse to visit and help me. But Verity didn't come.

There was only Maria. No wartime nightmares, no Mexican address, no haunting scent.

I took my first smoke to help me face the day and cope with the hangover.

Then it hit me. The shock, the anger at Flynn, and then the booze… They'd all fogged up my brain. It wasn't Maria on that bed. It was Isabella.

Maria'd grabbed the only valuable thing in her life—the photo—and fled. God knew where to. I had to pray she was safe.

But another innocent girl had died. Who else would die because I wouldn't let go?

Was I going to quit the case, to follow orders, to forget the murders?

No. I had to see this through. Caldera would chase down Maria if he worked it out, too. He also knew about Mom and where she was.

I couldn't trust the Feds or the cops. I had to do this myself.

Lyra was right. It was down to me. Or who else might die?

23. A BLOND

"Is Jake around?" I'd called Myers' office. The voice on the phone wasn't Jake's. My hangover was easing. My guilt wasn't.

"Not right now. He's…occupied. I'm his brother, Adam. How can I help you?" He sounded distracted. I said Jake was doing some research for me and asked for him to call me back.

"I'm sorry, he can't do that. He was hit by a car. He's in the hospital. It'll be a while before he'll be back on the job. If it's urgent, I can take over, but you'll understand I have other priorities right now."

I gave him my sympathies and said it could wait. "You'd better make out my bill, you know, to help with the medical costs." It sounded clumsy. He seemed to take it as well meant.

Afterward, I tapped my fingers on the desk for a while. Accident? Coincidence? It stank. It stank of the Mansion. How did they know about Jake Myers? I remembered that Fed, probably Dutch, asking around Tahoe about the cabin fire. Reno was Mobland. They'd have eyes and ears everywhere. I'd been stupid. Fed informers, Mob informers: the same people double-dipping on the payoffs.

I was right—I couldn't trust anyone.

I needed answers, and I knew where to get them.

————

I parked up opposite the Bureau building. It was just before lunchtime. Dutch was a man of habit. He always ate out. I knew he didn't see much of his wife's cooking, and his waitress friend's specialty didn't lie in the kitchen. He was easy to spot with that blond hair, even in the dark suit they all liked to wear. He paused on the steps to put on his sunglasses. I pulled across the street to the sidewalk and threw open the passenger door. "Hi, Dutch. Hop in."

There it was again, that nervous glancing around. But he didn't have much choice without drawing more attention. He climbed in.

"Hello, Sarge. Why the ride?" He showed no sign of pleasure at seeing me.

"Lunch." As I pulled away, he looked back over his shoulder. This man was real nervous around me. No point wasting time. "So tell me, Dutch. Why am I such bad news these days? And don't shake your head. I got you, the LAPD, the Bayville Sheriff, and the Mob all warning me off. Tell me what I'm supposed to stay away from, Dutch, and why."

"Drop me at the corner."

"Nope." I pressed the gas pedal a little harder. "Someone from the office must have seen you get in. If I'm on someone's list, you already got some explaining to do back there, I guess. Anyway, we're headed way out of town. It'll be a long lunch break for you. Unless you want to leave a moving vehicle at speed." I drove on, heading north and west, until his face showed me he'd realized I was serious. Still, he held his silence.

"Dutch, if I find out for myself, I'll finger you. We've been seen together twice. It'll hold up. If you tell me, I'll keep you out of it."

He thought about it.

I turned the screw a bit more. "The other day, I asked about your family. You told me a nice story about Lilly and the kids. You didn't mention Conchita."

"Son of a bitch!"

"Remember Conchita? Pretty little Mexican girl? Came as a *bracero* worker and somehow got fake papers to stay longer? Remember?"

He fell into silence.

"By the way, does Lilly know about Conchita? Probably does. Staying quiet for the kids' sakes. But does the Bureau know who got her those fake papers?" He glared at me. I waited for his anger to die down and the message to sink in. "So tell me why the Mansion is hands off." I leaned on the gas pedal.

"Listen, I can't say much." He waited for me to accept it. I said nothing, letting him do the talking.

"There are some cases we don't chase, because they have wider implications. You know, let the sprat go and wait for the mackerel?"

"A sprat? I don't consider a major gambling, drugs, and pros-titution ring a sprat. Sounds more like a whale. I need better than that. You keep talking or I keep driving and later I'll call Lilly and the Bureau." I leaned on the gas a little more, risking a speeding ticket. "Remember the Senator Booth shooting you were involved in and the whole Joey Milan thing? That was all covered up. Maybe someone should…"

"The Mansion. Okay, stop the car." He got nothing from me but another tap on the gas pedal. "Damn it, at least slow down." He looked miserable.

"If I get stopped for speeding, you can always flash your Bureau badge. And just hope the speed cop doesn't log it."

"Look, there's wider implications. I can't give you details."

"Wider implications, eh? Like letting movietown's rich and beautiful and their money-men get away scot-free again?"

"Damn it, a public bust would destroy too many careers. You want a ghost town on the coast? All those jobs lost?"

I already knew Caldera's Mob had fingers in the studios. "So it's political? Taxpayers paying for you to make sure the tax dollars keep rolling in from the theater ticket sales?" I glanced over at him, sitting with a long face and clenched teeth. "You're never going to take them down, are you?"

Like a broken dam, his story all poured out in a flood. "Caldera doesn't own the operation. He just runs it. When the last manager died—"

"Joey Milan."

"Yeah, Milan." He spoke through gritted teeth. "We ran his Mob out of town. Reno took over. Brought Caldera in. We've no history on him. He's the sprat. We want to get the syndicate behind it, close 'em down permanent."

"And movietown's biggest and brightest being Mansion clients counts for nothing when you think about priorities?"

"I told you, we're waiting for the right moment. We know Caldera flies to meet the Reno syndicate at irregular intervals. We want to grab the whole bunch at the meeting place, away from the spotlight, the press, you know?"

"They meet at Reno? Why haven't you grabbed the syndicate when they meet? I know Reno's in Nevada, not California, but you're the Feds. Crossing state lines is what you're for."

"No, he flies to Sky Harbor field, near Lake Tahoe. Usually near month end, but never the same date. The syndicate meets up at one of their Reno casino hotels. We know where. We just don't know when. We don't have the numbers to keep a day and night watch on him."

Justification and excuses. The Feds were never going to intervene.

"We want to grab the capo and his top soldiers at the same time. Maybe the bookkeeper, too."

Yeah, yeah. Nice story. No studio would buy a script as crummy as that. Neither would I.

Dutch changed tack. "You know, Sarge, old war buddies ought to stick together?" It made me sick to hear a war veteran whine.

I had other ideas. "I think there's more. Thought I'd go pick up Conchita and introduce her to your wife then give her a lift over to Immigration."

"You know I'm not going to let you do that." He pulled back his jacket to display his shoulder holster.

"No? Okay, I'll bring your wife to the bar one night." I didn't need to see his sweat; I could almost smell it. I pushed harder. "Or we could drive out to the Mansion now and I could introduce you to the capo there. Unless he already knows you?"

"Damn you!" He reached inside his jacket.

"Don't be stupid." I hit the gas again. "Leave the heat where it is. We're nearly done."

His face hung so low, he couldn't see I'd turned around and was heading back to the Bureau. "It's planned, Sarge. Soon. As soon as we get the next meet date." It must have sounded pathetic, even to him.

No, the Feds were never going to act. Someone else had to.

"By the way, that rusty-head's gone away since I mentioned him to you."

"Listen, lay off, Sarge. Stay away. Just a bit longer. Then you can chase up your dead girl."

Now how did he know about that? "Which one?"

"Oh, God. There's more than one? Listen, you have to get out of this. Drop whatever you're doing. Take a vacation."

"I might just do that. I hear Lake Tahoe's good this time of year." That looked like horror on his face. "So what's Sheriff Jackson's interest?"

A long pause. He surrendered. "A father's shame. And politics. He didn't want anyone to know what his sweet little girl had gotten into. Cut her out of his life. Didn't want to upset the voters. Didn't want to risk his career. And maybe there's a cash payoff, I don't know." He looked around like he was waking from a nightmare, realized where he was, on the street where I'd picked him up. "Let me out. I'm saying nothing more. You have no idea what you're mixed up in, who you're upsetting. Believe me, it's just bad news for you from now on. I'll have to tell my superiors about this."

"Conchita." It was all I needed to say. "I hope your empty stomach doesn't rumble too loud all afternoon." I coasted slowly along the street. There was one last question, an afterthought. "Did Harry do the artwork on those fake papers?"

He nodded sharply, gnawing at his lip. I never saw a man in a nice dark suit and a spotless white shirt look more pathetic.

I pulled over. "Dutch, you were a lousy soldier and now you're a lousy husband and a lousy agent. Get out."

———

Mid-afternoon, Adam Myers rang from Reno. "I wanted to make out your bill, and I checked Jake's files. He's a fiend about filing, but there's nothing under your name. I don't know what work we did for you."

"Any other files missing?" I already knew what he'd say. Nothing else had gone. "Listen, he checked out some records for me, made a couple of visits. Bill me for three days now and for any extra if Jake says so. I'll play fair." I was feeling generous with Lyra's Benjamins.

Car accident and missing files? I sighed. I'd already guessed why Jake had been run down. Now I knew for sure. I had another person's blood on my hands.

The FBI was sitting on its hands while people died.

I'd had enough.

But so had someone else.

My thoughts were turning over plans, hopeless plans. I knew I had to act, to protect those I loved. But how? I couldn't take Caldera out at the Mansion; I'd never get close enough with a weapon.

I'd reached my car when they jumped me. Marty stepped out from behind a truck with Nameless close behind, waving an automatic. So much for my plans. A redheaded guy wearing a loud tie hovered in the background.

I nodded to myself and raised my hands. "Evening, fellas. Can I help you? You lost? Need directions?"

"No, bub. You the one that's lost." Marty grabbed my arm and twisted it high up my back, pushing me, forcing me into an alley. Nameless kept a safe distance, covering me. I didn't feel it would be polite to resist.

Marty growled in my ear. "You guys never listen. You got the warning, you got the payoff, you shoulda stayed away. But oh, no. You're too damn stupid. You had to go see Viola Firenze and go asking around Tahoe. So we wasted the whore like he told you we would, and—for a bonus, just in case that ain't enough—we gonna make sure you really learn your lesson. Boss says pain lasts longer than a quick slug between the eyes. He kinda enjoys hurting people, you know? But next time, there won't be any pain, just a big bang and your brains all over the wall. Sound familiar?"

The powerful ape-grip jerked my arm higher so I had to lean forward. That's when Nameless came close, and something slammed against the back of my head.

It felt just like the automatic I'd seen him holding.

Lights flashed. Stars burned themselves out behind my eyelids. The darkness deepened. I was out.

———

I woke. I really hadn't expected to. I guessed my winning charm saved me. But there wasn't a part of my body that didn't scream pain. I'd had a serious working-over after I passed out.

I tried opening one eye. Mistake. Streetlight glare sliced into my brain. I snapped it shut. Looking around could wait. My whole body ached, but my head and chest had priority. I reached around and tested my scalp for blood. It hurt to touch. The blood was caked. I heard traffic. I risked another peek. I was in the passenger seat of my car, parked up on some street I didn't recognize.

A door opened in a nearby apartment block. A woman stepped out. She was familiar, but parts of my brain weren't working right. She came closer. Her face showed she knew me. Young, pretty, mousy hair, brown eyes behind unflattering spectacle frames… Her puzzled expression changed to horror. I saw her mouth shaping, "My God!" She jerked open my door. "Are you all right? What happened?"

"Good evening, Miss Grey." I tried to smile, but it felt more like a grimace. I keeled over out of the seat and into the street. I went back to the dark place.

24. ANOTHER PUPPET

I surfaced from a dark well of pain that didn't lift as I took in my surroundings.

Bedroom. Not mine. Closed window drapes. A soft, comfortable bed and the scent of flowers. Not a hospital. I heard a gasp nearby and turned my head sharply. The pain made me regret it. Donna sat next to the bed, wound up like a spring, hands clasped so tight her knuckles were white. She fumbled for something to say, her mouth trying a few starts before settling for, "Are you all right? What happened?"

Didn't someone say that a few minutes ago?

So they knew where she lived. Even I hadn't known. They'd known about Maria and about Mom's residential home. Now Donna. I got the message. The three most important women in my life. They'd made the hit at Maria's place. Sounded like they didn't know yet it wasn't her. Mom was surrounded by staff, and a hit on her would be too public. I hoped.

They'd said it would be me next time. But I still worried about Donna and Mom and Maria.

They had my strings in their hands. I was another puppet. Bringing me here was a heavy reminder of how powerful they were. They knew everything about me and who I knew. I'd never escape them if I tried anything else. Mental pain to add to my body's damage.

Backtrack. Did I just say Donna was one of the three most important people to me?

I looked down. I was in pale blue pajamas like I wore as a kid. "How'd I get here?"

"Oh, a neighbor helped bring you up and I changed you into some nightwear he lent me. I didn't have pajamas that would fit you."

Raising my eyebrows cost me a lot of pain. "I did wonder why you had gent's pajamas around the place."

She flushed the sweetest shade. "Oh, no. I said they're not mine. I mean, there's no man, I don't, no one…" Her voice trailed off in pink embarrassment.

"It's okay." I wanted to pat her arm, but that seemed too kinda personal…too intimate.

"But," she said, her gaze fixed on her shoes, "I do wear them myself. Just a smaller size—" Donna was rambling.

Time for me to change the subject or leave. "I have to go." I tried to sit up. I failed. The pain.

She rested a hand on my chest. It felt good. I wanted it to last. "You stay right there. I called in some unused vacation so I can look after you."

I wanted nothing more than having Donna look after me.

"I called a doctor. He said you had concussion from a heavy blow to the skull. You have two bruised ribs, and your body is covered in bruises. He taped up your chest and left a prescription for painkillers. He wanted to call the police. I thought you should decide. He said if you didn't wake soon or if you were confused when you did, I should call an ambulance. Shall I?"

"How long have I been under?"

"A couple of hours."

"I'm okay. I fell down a flight of stairs."

"How many times?" She looked incredulous.

I put on as much honesty as I could muster. "Two or three. I'll be fine. I just need to rest for a while."

"You have bruises all over your body and ribs!"

"It was a tall flight of stairs."

She scowled but let me run with that story for now. "How many fingers am I holding up?"

I guessed. "One."

"Close enough." She smiled. "I'll make soup. You just lay there and enjoy being pampered. I'll leave the door open. Call if you need anything."

I thought about her offer. Nice thoughts. Then my ribs screamed at me. I pushed the pain away.

Pampered? I really felt like I could handle a lot of pampering right now. But I slipped into darkness again before the soup arrived. I slept a lot over the next twenty-four hours.

I checked the bruises when I was alone. Marty and Nameless had given me a real good going-over. No wonder the doc was concerned. And Donna had seen the damage when she changed my clothes. But she hadn't challenged my lie.

She also hadn't mentioned those fingernail scratches on my back.

Yeah, Donna was sweet.

Next day, the doctor visited and asked what year it was, who was president, if I felt nausea or dizziness… Donna had already run through this whole routine. I got all the answers right again, but I heard him whisper to her to call if I got worse.

I wanted to be up and back at the office but couldn't work out what I'd do if I did.

So I stayed put for a couple of days and tried to think it through. There was a lot to think through, but it still didn't hang together. I was missing some hook. I needed Verity to prompt me, but she didn't come to me, and I couldn't go to her.

Donna slept on the sofa in her living room. She left the door ajar so she could hear me if I called out. Through the narrow gap, I caught occasional glimpses of her moving about. She wore the cutest pink-and-white candy-striped pajamas, just like she'd said. They were a bit big for her; they hung loose. I liked it. Her glasses were off, and her hair was down. It was just a few glimpses. It made me want to see more.

She'd asked what this was all about. Was it a case? I owed her some explanation. So I talked about it a little. Just a little. I said I had a difficult client called Lyra who wanted me to find someone and it had just gone sour.

"Interesting name. It's a constellation, a group of stars." Donna was a box of brains.

Lyra wasn't just a star in star town; she was a whole bunch of stars.

"Also a lyre, a stringed musical instrument." She grinned. "The way you talk about her, it sounds as if she's plucking your strings. Are you her puppet?"

Was that jealousy?

I remembered a viola was a stringed musical instrument, too.

"And, of course," she talked on past the moment, "the name sounds like 'liar.' So which is she? A bundle of stars, a puppeteer, or a liar?"

"All three." I knew what Lyra was to me. It hit me that Lyra-liar balanced Verity-truth. Jimmy'd said *"in vino veritas"* before handing me over to Verity. It all hurt my head.

I changed the subject. "So what brought you to movietown?"

She shrugged. "Work." It was too vague. I waited for more. There was no more. I didn't press the point. She'd earned her privacy.

I gave her a nod and pleaded tiredness. "Oh, one last thing, what's a nemesis?"

She smiled. "Nemesis was female, the Greek goddess of inescapable justice and divine retribution." She chuckled as she adjusted the pillow. "That role sounds a bit pompous for you. Now lie back and rest."

Easier said than done. I was damaged but not broken. Donna bent low over me as she worked on the pillow. I just had to lift my back off the bed a little and wrap my arms around her…

Maybe she caught me preparing to move. She pulled back a little, pressed her fingers against my chest, and smiled a gentle smile. "Not yet." It was a whisper. Then she was gone.

———

Donna insisted I rest up for longer than I wanted. Inaction frustrated me, but I was happy in her care and in her company. I still couldn't work out what I'd do if I went back to the case. There didn't seem to be a case anymore. I had two consolations: being pampered by Donna and knowing I'd been on the button about the case. Trouble was I didn't know what the button was, and I had to button my lip about it. Now that's a tricky act to pull off.

Having her so close all the time but out of reach frustrated me a helluva lot more. Maybe when I was recovered…?

I gave her my keys so she could pick up some kit from my apartment—clothes, smokes…

Later, she stood by the bed, emptying a valise of my stuff, all neatly folded. She kept her gaze down. She had something on her mind. I let it brew. She'd say it when she was ready, whatever it was. Then she blurted it out. "I saw the medals."

I shrugged.

"Oh, don't think I searched your place." She looked horrified at the thought. "Just looked in your closet. For clothes."

"Sure. They were in the sock drawer. You brought socks."

"But those medals! Purple Heart, Silver Star, and the rest."

"Yeah. Those are medals."

"They should be displayed proudly, not hidden away." She looked down, like she was pulling herself together. "And I saw the scar. The bullet wound. On your chest. When we changed your clothes. I tried not to look…" A pink tinge touched her cheeks. "But I wondered. Wondered if it was the war or the job."

"Long ago and far away. Forget it." I tried to sound casual.

"Have *you* forgotten? It must have been terrible."

I lost my amiability. "I said forget it." It came out as a growl.

She looked like I'd slugged her then headed for the bathroom. She was in there a long time. I didn't disturb her.

I looked through the stuff remaining in the valise. No smokes.

If a dame wasn't trying to manipulate you, she was trying to mother you.

After a few days, she agreed to go back to work and leave me to potter about the place in those pajamas and her bathrobe whose belt didn't quite fasten around me. I clutched the front closed and felt like an old man. My pain made me feel like one, too. I told her I was thinking clearly, no confusion, no dizziness. She believed me. She wanted to, I guess.

While she was out, I took a look around her home. Tidy, of course. Lots of books, of course. Tasteful, subdued, calm.

Donna wouldn't bring me any smokes, so I searched for my clothes to go buy some. I really wasn't looking for anything personal about her. Innocent Donna Grey? What could there possibly be to find out?

So what I found in the drawers hit me in the gut. A driver's license for Joan Watts. Graduation papers in that name. I dug deeper in the paperwork. A yearbook with Donna's photo bearing the same name.

Damnation! Just like every other woman in my life, Donna—Joan—was a fake.

Maybe I should've guessed. Good things didn't happen to me. And Donna was such a damn good thing.

Maybe everyone had secrets. Maybe I could live with hers. Maybe not.

Only time would tell.

25. TAHOE

Donna sat on the arm of the easy chair, spoon-feeding me. I could handle a spoon fine, but why fight a good thing? It was a special meal she was real proud of. Tasted like heaven. I could do with a cook like her at home. I could get used to being pampered.

Dangerous thoughts!

I'd pushed down my doubts about her and was enjoying the present moment. So she had a degree or two. So she used a different name. Nothing I'd learned said Joan Watts was anything other than an egghead who—for her own reasons—wanted to pose as librarian Donna Grey. Maybe the academic life was too stressful. What the hell did I know about it? It was her business. To me, she was sweet, innocent, caring…and maybe a little sweet on me.

I could live with that.

"You're very quiet." A cute little frown creased her forehead.

"I'm thinking." It was true.

"About what?"

"Tahoe." It was a lie.

"It's to do with the men who beat you up, isn't it? It's dangerous." She rested her hand on mine, worry written across her face.

"Donna, it's dangerous to a lot of people. But the danger stays, even if I back off. They can hurt people I'm fond of, anytime." I didn't say "people like you."

I tried to explain. "I'd be a puppet forever. I'm not a man to roll over and play dead on command. Not good at following orders."

She examined my face, speaking slow and calm with the hint of a smile. "I don't suppose you are. But you're injured. And it's more dangerous to go than to do nothing, I can tell."

"I am going to Lake Tahoe."

Donna took a long time to explain how deeply and in how many ways quite how insane I was. She used lots of fancy words, too.

"Tahoe." I raised myself from the easy chair, head bent low to hide my grimace.

"You are in no state to drive for ten, perhaps twelve, hours. And not through the night." She watched me sway a little, her eyes widening. "You really mean it, don't you?"

I headed for the door, limping just a little. She grabbed my arm, turned me to face her, then supported me as I wobbled.

"You really mean to go!" That was real horror on her face.

She deserved an explanation. Half of one, at least. "Lyra mentioned Tahoe. I've seen a photo of a cabin there in Caldera's office. The cabin burned down, and some people died." That's all she needed to know for now. "It's important I go there, but I don't know why yet. Someone tried to kill a good guy up there who was helping me. People are threatening me and those around me, and I guess the next time they show, they'll just take me out of the picture. But I'm damned sure the answer is at Tahoe. I'm not going to let it go."

Why was that photo in Caldera's office? Maybe he liked the view? Or could Caldera actually feel guilty, despite his cold heart play?

He and Firenze were soldiers for the same Mob and of similar ages. They must've known each other. Old buddies, maybe close buddies, in the past, but orders were orders. When Firenze pissed off the local boys somehow, Caldera swapped a friend's life for a big reward. What's the scripture? "Greater love hath no man than this, that a man lay down his friend's life for lakeside real estate and a plum job?" Something like that.

I was missing something. Memories lost in a painkiller fog in my brain…

"You are so darn stubborn." Donna almost stamped her foot. The cuteness of that "darn" really got to me. "If you must go, I'll drive you." She waved away my objections and listed her reasons. "The roads might be still washed out after the August floods. I still have unused vacation, and I need a break." Her voice softened. "Anyway, I hear it's nice at Tahoe. And I will not let you go alone." She blocked my path and showed a determination I'd never seen before. She wasn't just a cute puppy. But I already knew there was more to her than appearances.

She'd said "nice at Tahoe?" Burned cabins, charred bodies, lying witnesses, dangerous drivers, missing files… Yep, it sure did sound nice at Tahoe. I didn't want to involve her in the risk, but it looked like she was already involved. "Okay, you can drive." She was right. I couldn't make it alone. "But you stay in the motel."

"Agreed. In my own room."

I sighed. She sounded like she meant it. But I guessed I needed to get this case closed one way or the other before I made a serious move on her.

"And perhaps I shall get some sunshine." She caught my glance. "But only in the forecourt." She finished in a hurry. "I'll call in some more vacation, should be no problem, they owe me, and we can set off in the morning."

"Okay. We'll stay somewhere south of the lake, out of town. I'll visit the cabin and a couple of other places. Should take a day, maybe two, four including the drive." I also needed to get home for cash and more clothes and then to drop by the office. I didn't tell Donna it was to collect my spare gun, an efficient Luger I'd souvenired from the Rhine, or about the smokes I needed.

I watched her packing for the journey like it was a joyride. Singing a little song to herself, holding up this blouse and that skirt, asking my approval.

It was like being married again.

The early days, at least.

I woke as the car pulled into a motel forecourt. "Where are we?"

"Just south of Tahoe according to the map. About an hour from Reno. Is this suitable?" The motel was newish but basic. Across the street, a truck-stop diner was still open. It was good enough.

A skinny, middle-aged motel clerk shuffled out from the back office when I hit the bell. I asked for two rooms. He peered over his glasses, looking from me to Donna, and shook his head in disbelief as he made a ritual out of examining the register. "Just the one twin room left." He didn't seem to think he was disappointing us.

I glanced at Donna. "We'll drive on, then. Know anywhere—"

"One room is fine," she interrupted. "We're tired. We need to rest."

"I'll take the sofa, then."

"You most certainly will not do any such thing!"

The clerk interrupted. "We got twin beds. So will you lovebirds be taking the room or no? My supper's getting cold."

I yielded. And I would have another chance to see Donna take off her glasses and let down her hair. "I snore," I warned her.

"I know. You've been sleeping at my place for a week, and

you snored in the car for four hundred miles." Donna produced an infectious grin that lifted my spirits.

The clerk looked bored. He interrupted again, shoving the register at me across the counter. "Welcome to the Nevada Road-side Motel."

I sighed and signed. He glanced at the names I'd written as he handed us the keys. "Mr. and Mrs. Smith. Glad your marital dispute was sorted out so fast. Lord, we do get a lot of folks named Smith these days." His bored expression never changed. "Anyways, enjoy your stay. I'm off back to enjoy what's left of my supper."

The room was as expected. Comfortable enough without luxury. There were, as promised, twin beds. I let Donna choose.

We decided to skip dinner. I let her shower first. I'd forgotten how long that took a woman. She emerged wearing a white cotton bathrobe over her candy-stripe pajamas, drying her long hair with a towel and avoiding my eyes. Her cheeks carried an adorable blush, maybe brought on by the hot water, maybe not. I guessed we were both uncomfortable with the sleeping arrange-ments. Sure, I'd spent a few nights in her bed, but there'd been a wall between us. This was very different, a new level of intimacy.

She was asleep before I'd finished showering. She must've been exhausted from the drive. I lay in bed listening to her steady, shallow breathing. I whispered a goodnight and killed the lights. I lay awake a long time, thinking over the last couple of weeks, the days ahead, and wondering why in hell's name I'd allowed her to come along. Of course, I hadn't had any choice in the matter. Strong-willed woman, my Donna.

Did I just call her "my" Donna?

For another thing, I enjoyed her company. For another, I wanted her close so I could keep her out of danger here, far from the Mansion and its corruption.

———

Sunlight lit up the thin drapes at dawn, waking us both. We took turns dressing in the bathroom then strolled across the tarmac to the diner. It served the worst breakfast I ever ate, washed down by the worst coffee I ever drank. Even worse than field rations. I kept an eye open for anyone who might be keeping an eye open for us. The only other customer was a trucker trying his luck with the waitress.

Donna looked stunning. It wasn't just the fresh sunshine lighting up her face and hair, which she'd left hanging down to her shoulders. She seemed to be lit up from inside, excited by the adventure she was on. All I had to do was to keep her safe. That's all.

We made a little small talk as we breakfasted. I asked again what brought her to movietown and what she'd done before.

She told me how she was from a small Pennsylvania town where nothing ever happened. "One of those hick towns no one's ever heard of." She loved reading and learning facts, did well at school, came to LA for the big city and the sunny beaches.

It didn't ring true. It was a well-rehearsed story. She wasn't a beach girl; she wasn't a party girl. She'd banked weeks of unused vacation. She seemed to have no friends. Donna was keeping a low profile and hiding behind the heavy frames of the glasses she didn't need.

Yeah, I'd checked when she was in the shower. The lenses were plain glass.

So I told her about a quarter of my life story and all of it true. She listened fascinated as I talked about Mom, the farm I was born on, the drive west, the army... She didn't ask questions, didn't probe deeper. I guessed she didn't want me probing back.

We didn't wait around to see if the trucker had any success with the waitress. I doubt he did. I glanced over the few other cars parked at the motel and the diner. None had California plates. I relaxed a little.

We'd come to see the cabin. Myers had given me the address. Donna looked out at the sunny day and insisted on driving. I weighed up the risks: to be seen with me or to be left alone? Hell, they already knew about her, where she lived, probably where she worked.

But did they know everything about her?

I'd mulled it over a lot in the past few days and decided she was on my side. Nothing said she wasn't. I didn't want her to not be. So, like any guy with a beautiful, caring female companion who was not what she seemed, I went with my gut and decided to enjoy the ride while it lasted.

I felt she'd be safer where I could keep an eye on her and she could do the driving. Riding shotgun gave me the chance to gaze out at the famous scenery. It didn't impress. Miles and miles of dark green pines, standing tall and stiff. Give me LA's swaying palms any day.

26. ILLUMINATION

We cruised north to the lake and turned north-east toward Reno. It really was a fine day with a great view of the sparkling lake. Forest hugged its shoreline and spread over the hills into the hazy distance.

It was almost like we were on vacation. I actually felt my face distort into a stupid smile.

The road followed the edge of a small bay then curved inland. The trees blocked our view of the water. I was sure this was the estate, the cabin grounds. A rusted iron fence ran for a mile or so. We almost missed the gateway, it was so overgrown. Donna screeched to a halt when I called out and reversed into the roadside. Two moss-covered stone columns served as gateposts. The iron gates hung half-open and trapped in the undergrowth. There wasn't enough gap to get a car through. I hadn't brought jungle-clearing gear. We'd have to walk.

I climbed out, hiding the pain it cost me, and took a look. Weeds and low bushes were taking over a gravel driveway that led deeper into the trees. I couldn't see any buildings from here.

Donna joined me and stood close, waiting. My hand wanted to take hold of hers for our stroll through the forest. I didn't let it.

I led the way along the gravel way until we stepped out into an open area at the lakeside.

And there it was. The cabin.

To me, a cabin in the forest was four walls made of interlocking logs and shutters with heavy drapes on the windows to keep the draughts out. But I was moving in better circles these days. This place was more like a real house: a real big house bought by real big money. I guessed you could have fitted the whole floor of my apartment block inside it. From the stubs of fallen walls marking the rooms, I guessed six or more bedrooms with a broad communal area.

Once, there'd have been a neatly cropped lawn, flower beds, window boxes… Now there were just weeds and untended grasses. Nature had taken back control. Or maybe it was just being disobedient with no people around to punish it.

I clambered among the ruins, nosing around.

She grabbed my arm. "Do be careful."

"Thanks. I wasn't going to be. But just for you, I will."

Between the pain in my ribs and the uncertain ground underfoot, I didn't need Donna's advice. But it was nice to know she cared.

The cabin stood on a gentle rise, giving a lake view worth every cent paid for it, no matter how much that was. Thrusting out from the shoreline was a familiar jetty. A shiver ran down my back. I was standing in the exact spot where the photo had been taken.

This was the view that hung on Caldera's wall and stood on Lyra's dresser. It just lacked the woman in white.

"Are you all right?" Donna's fingertips touched my hand. "You look terrible. Oh, you're ice cold!"

I shook off the mood but not the contact. "Sure. I'm fine. Let's explore." I stepped away before she could follow through.

The collapsed roof had brought down part of the floor. A large basement area was now open to the sky. Rafters, blackened, weathered, and moss-covered, jutted like ribs toward the clear blue above. Amid the debris, I made out the remains of some wooden structures—the furniture of wine storage or of torture? I couldn't tell. I didn't want to.

We spotted the shriveled remains of wrapped flowers tucked deep into a gap in the broken wall. Two bunches. One for each year since Verity died.

My attention kept drifting toward the jetty. I couldn't put it off any longer. Anyway, there wasn't much more to see at the cabin. I led. Donna followed.

I got my first close-up look at the jetty. I froze. It was almost a dead ringer for the pier at Jimmy's Bar. Wooden planks jutted out over water.

A second look showed me it wasn't. Corruption was spreading. Some planks had rotted and fallen into the water. Moss crept up from the water's surface along all the support posts. There was no sign of a boat. Lost, taken to safety, stolen? Who could tell?

But before the fire, it'd have been a damn close enough family likeness.

I still wasn't sure if I should tell Donna about Verity. Would she think I was crazy? I was becoming convinced I was.

I had to take a smoke, ignoring Donna's disapproving face. I felt something I couldn't name—a presence and an absence, like I was so damn close to Verity, but so far away.

There was nothing else to see, so I dragged myself away.

———

We drove down to Jake's hospital in Reno. His brother had told me the incident was listed as an accident, so there was no police guard. I didn't like that. Anyone could come and go as they wanted. Anyone except Jake, of course, with his leg plastered up and hanging high, strung on straps to the ceiling. He welcomed us warmly, in a room filled with flowers and get-well cards. Jake seemed to be a popular guy.

He was a rugged, clean-cut jock. Square chin, deep brown eyes... a handsome ex-marine. Too handsome for my liking.

We shook, and I introduced Donna. He held onto her handshake longer than mine. He seemed more interested in her than in me. I liked him a little less than before.

She sat on the single visitor chair. I perched on the windowsill.

Jake kept his eyes on Donna. At least she was brightening up his day. "So what brings you all this way north? I know it wasn't just to bring me flowers."

"Flowers? Oh, yeah. Sorry."

He grinned and waved a hand to dismiss my apology.

I told him most of the story, just enough. Nothing about my talks with Verity—I didn't want him thinking I was crazy. Not very much about Maria. Nothing about the night with Lyra. After all, Donna was hearing all this for the first time as well. Talking about ghost women, hooker girlfriends, and sleeping with my client? Didn't feel right to share everything.

"Which date was marked on Caldera's calendar?" This was Donna. Cutting to the chase faster than a couple of two-bit investigators.

"Twentieth."

"Today, then?"

"Twentieth today?" I'd lost track of time while I lounged about in bed. Damnation!

Now I knew why I was here, *had* to be here.

That red circle on the wall calendar—the twentieth, the anniversary of the fire.

This was the end.

I'd decided.

Donna and my mom were at risk, and Maria if they found her. I was certain they wouldn't just take me out, but they'd clear the decks of everyone close to me.

It had to end tonight.

I stood and blurted out, "The Mob meeting's today. Caldera's already here in Reno." I bit back the rest of it.

I knew where he'd be after the Mob meeting. There were dead flowers at the cabin. One bundle for each anniversary of the fire. It could only be Caldera. Yes, that cold bastard's heart *could* feel guilt, after all. And he would be at the cabin again today, after the business meeting, I guessed.

I had to go there and fast.

And close this case, just the way Lyra had wanted.

27. LOSING DONNA

I grabbed Donna's hand. "Come. Quick."

"Catch you later, Jake," I called over my shoulder as we hit the hallway.

I dragged her out to the parking lot. She didn't resist. Not until we reached the car.

She shook her hand free, folded her arms, and dug her heels in beside the driver's door. "Tell me what just happened."

We were inches apart.

"Caldera's going to be at the cabin tonight."

"And?"

I took a deep breath to calm down. Mistake. I got a double-barreled shot of her soft perfume. I took a pause.

"I'm waiting."

I loved it when she got all fired up, her vulnerability wiped away, but still my Donna underneath it all.

"You're going back to the motel. I'm not taking you with me for this. Don't argue."

Donna was Donna. She argued.

"I am not. You're still injured. You're angry. Not thinking straight. I'm not stupid. You're going to kill a man, to murder him. That's not you. You're a good man. I don't want to even think of you doing that."

A good man? She sounded like my mother! I waited till she took a breath. Her face grew flushed, and her eyes sparkled.

"I said not to argue. I'm doing this. You're not coming with me." I wrenched the door open and slid into the driver seat. "Motel or stay here. Choose."

Donna glared at me but for only a second or two. She scooted round the passenger side and clambered in. "Motel. I can pack and find out how to get back to LA when you don't come back." She tried to sound like she didn't care.

Handling the gearshift hurt my ribs, but worse was the freeze-out. She was showing me ice-queen Donna, sitting stubborn, gaze fixed on the road ahead.

I was watching out for patrol cars that might notice my speed, trying to focus on the night to come and not on her pain. It was a silent ride.

She spoke just once. "You're really going to kill him, aren't you? If he doesn't kill you first." Donna sounded disappointed. She turned to face me. "Listen, you're no murderer." She turned back to face the road ahead. "And I don't want to lose you."

That last part hurt so bad. It sounded like she was fighting back tears.

I forced my eyes to stay on the road I didn't really see anymore. I couldn't bear to look at her.

Neither of us spoke again until we reached the motel. I still didn't look at her, was afraid I'd see tears. I pulled in right outside our room.

Time pressed on me. Twilight was creeping in from the east.

"I want you to go away." I didn't sound convincing even to me. "Where you'll be safe." That came out better.

Without a word or a glance, she gathered her things and climbed out the car. She slammed the door hard. I felt the impact deep inside me.

I should have driven away, but I just had to watch her stride toward our motel room.

My mind was wrapped up in the events to come and on the distress of the girl I loved.

Love? Damn! I'd used the word—*that* word—but just to myself. She wouldn't know. But what the hell was I doing?

Let's say I was kinda distracted. So I almost missed what happened.

She grabbed the door handle and walked straight in without a backward glance.

That wasn't right.

The key was in my pocket.

But the door was not locked.

I scrambled out the car and drew my Luger as I raced after her.

I kicked it open and charged through.

Donna stood between the beds, her hands raised. Marty stood right next to her, his automatic's barrel resting against her forehead.

"Don't do nothing stupid, pal. Not unless you want another pretty girlfriend's face spread across a bedroom wall." God, how I hated that sneer on his thuggish face.

I couldn't risk a shot. I could take him down, but a reflex finger-tightening on the trigger would fire his gun. Slowly, I snicked the safety on, tossed my Luger onto the bed, and raised my hands.

I knew he'd come to kill us both, but I had to delay until I could think of something. Something. Anything.

Marty chuckled like a cat choking. He turned his aim at me and stepped forward. "Well, at last I get to deal with you properly. No more threats. No more payoffs. No more gentle beatings. You just had to play hero for a pretty face." He was enjoying his moment of triumph, stretching it out, watching me suffer. "And later, me and the dame'll have some fun. Yeah, cutie?"

Donna lowered her hands and stared at me. I couldn't read her expression. The blood drained from my life.

Marty stepped closer to me, holding the pistol steady. "So, *Mr. Lake*, you screwed up big time. Boss'll do his flower drop and cry a bit, then get back to work. You'll be out of the way. No more brandy and guilt sessions. You know, he was pretty okay till you walked in. It'll be good to get back to the good old days, with you gone and not stirring up crap."

I was staring at Donna. She stood behind the guy who was going to kill me, the guy I'd tried to save her from. I already knew she wasn't really just a cute librarian tucked away in the archives.

Bait. Just beautiful and convincing bait.

I felt like I didn't have anything else to live for.

But how had they worked it? Meeting her was by chance. Wasn't it? But they'd known where she lived. They'd dropped me there. Did they recruit her later? Blackmail? Threats? Bribe? What? How? When?

I thought I knew her. I thought she meant it. I thought…

"Say goodbye to your sweetheart, pal. Time to go." My attention snapped back to Marty, a cruel smirk on his face. "We got plenty of time to have some fun after you've gone. Plenty of time." He laughed out loud.

I waited for the bang. No life-flashing-past-my eyes, I just froze. So this was how it ends: waiting for a bang.

I heard a crash.

Then a bang.

A slug slammed into the wall behind me. Marty's jaw fell open as his eyes rolled up into his head. The thug crumpled to the floor, his fingers slack, the pistol falling from his grasp.

Donna stood with the remains of a shattered bedside lamp in her hand and scattered ceramic shards around her feet. I hadn't seen her grab it. Marty certainly hadn't.

"Never underestimate a woman, you cretin." She threw the remains of her weapon down and rushed over to me, wrapping her arms round me and sobbing. She babbled, but I couldn't catch the words. I grabbed her upper arms and pushed her away. "Hold on."

Her face fell until she saw what I was doing.

I yanked the lamp's electric wire from the wall and tied Marty up real tight. Real tight. Welt-raising tight. A small gesture.

Then I took her in my arms. "For a minute there, I thought you were with them."

She tensed and pulled away. "You didn't think I was in league with them? And what that horrid man said about…" She shuddered then brightened. "So you were right. The gang boss *will* be at the cabin. Let's go."

Was there no end to this girl's optimism?

"No. I'll go. Go to reception and call the cops. Say he tried to rape you at gunpoint. Someone'll have heard the shot. They'll call it in, and the cops'll be looking for us soon anyway. Get the heat off my back."

"Give you time? Enough time to murder someone or be killed yourself?" I heard anger, disappointment, pain, despair. A real bad mix.

I gathered up my Luger. I left his Colt for the cops to find. "Enough time to bring this whole thing to an end."

"One way or the other?"

"Yes. One way or the other. But I'll be back. Stay here till the cops come then insist you go with them for safety. Cry and stuff."

She blinked at my last suggestion through a crestfallen face. Her shoulders sagged. She looked down at my shoes. "I'd hoped…" She pulled herself together. "When you told me how dirty and dangerous your work was, I didn't want to believe it. Now I do." She looked up at me, her eyes sparkling. "Come back to me?" She sounded like a little girl who'd been told Christmas was canceled.

I wanted to grab her, but a clock was ticking in the back of my mind. Maybe it'd be best to let things hang, especially as I might not be back. I pushed the thought down. "I *will* be back." It sounded firm. I was reassuring myself as well as her.

"Sounds like General MacArthur leaving the Philippines." Her face found a crooked smile. Her voice went pompous. "*I will return!*" I knew she was trying to lift the moment with some smart comedy. She smiled at me, a sad smile. That kid really hit me in the heart.

"And he *did* return." I slipped the Luger back into my shoulder holster. I grabbed her arms, held them tight, looked into her dark, brimming, brown eyes as I spoke. I wanted to throw her something to think about. "Listen, I'm not going to lose you. I just now felt what that'd be like. Not going to happen again."

I loosened my grip and let her go, turned, and left before she could get emotional.

And before I could plant a kiss on those beautiful, trembling lips.

28. DATE WITH DEATH

Caldera would be arriving from Reno. I drove up to the cabin from the Reno side and kept going. I looked for some pull-in after the cabin's gates where I could hide the car. I wanted this to be a surprise party.

Evening was creeping in by the time I hunkered down behind a tree near the cabin's overgrown driveway. The birds were falling silent. Bats fluttered in their dark hunt.

I settled in for a long wait, hunkered down against a pine in the undergrowth. My ribs ached. I thought about Donna. I pushed her out of my thoughts. I didn't want them to linger there.

I longed for a Lucky but couldn't risk anyone spotting the tip's glow or smelling smoke. It grew colder. I moved about a little to ease the stiffness, stretching my legs and arching my back. I had to be ready when he arrived.

The moon rose higher, playing hide-and-go-seek behind the clouds. A fan dancer giving her knowing smile: reveal, conceal, reveal, conceal…

I drifted off.

I jerked awake.

A car engine's roar. Headlamps flaring, lighting up the trees.

The car reached the driveway. I held myself ready. The sound dropped in tone, and the light faded as it roared past.

I watched the road for more approaching headlights. Another glow appeared. It got brighter. I tensed. The engine grew louder. The sound changed, the pitch droppinged. It sailed past, keeping its speed.

Wrong car again. I hunkered down again.

You know, it's funny how thoughts come to you when you're sitting in the dark, waiting, waiting…

All the bits and pieces of this mess started fitting together a different way. Lyra's lies, Verity's prompts…

But those prompts came from inside me, I was sure. No such things as ghosts!

Another hour. No more passing traffic. Nothing. Maybe I'd got it all wrong. Maybe I was on a wild goose chase. Maybe I was still chasing the ghosts I didn't believe in?

So I put it all together a different way, and the picture came out different. I knew now why I'd really come to Tahoe.

Again, the hint of headlamps' glow. Another passerby?

I stretched my stiff legs and arms, just in case. The engine noise rose. The glow grew brighter. The car slowed, pulled over into the old driveway entrance, and halted.

Bingo!

The lamps clicked off, leaving me in darkness again. I held position. It could be a courting couple in the wrong place at the wrong time. I peered through the tall weeds and untended bushes.

The interior car light flickered to life as the driver climbed out. It was enough to reveal one other occupant. A rear seat passenger. Caldera.

One mobster and one heavy. I liked those odds.

Caldera eased himself out and spoke to the driver. I couldn't make out the words. He set off through the overgrown darkness toward the ruins, cradling in the crook of his arm a bouquet of white lilies.

Funeral flowers.

I waited for the right moment, watching the driver. He reached into the car and clicked on the radio, leaving the door wide. A Zippo flared. I envied him for a moment, then I moved. He was leaning against the car, lost in the music or his thoughts or just enjoying the smoke.

It took just a few seconds. The music covered my footsteps. I was on him before he knew it, but my blow landed foul. He spun around, his cigarette's lit end tumbling into the grass. The idiot went for his gun instead of fighting back. My next two blows were solid, and he was down. I slammed the car door against his head, just to make sure.

There'd been hardly a sound, apart from the muffled door slam. I hoped Caldera was too far away to hear or too busy with his guilt and memories to take notice.

I checked the driver's pulse. Still there. His body driver fitted neatly into the trunk, trussed up with the tow rope he'd thought-fully packed, though I didn't expect him to move for a long time. I eased the lid shut with barely a click.

Now for Caldera.

Stepping as quiet as the training sergeant had drilled into us, I followed the gravel driveway after the man.

The moon chose to do a reveal right then. The light was good for me. Maybe the gods were on my side. I guessed Caldera knew the path well. I didn't. I needed the light. I wondered how long his guilt and grief would fill his attention.

And there he was, staring at the cabin's blackened bones in the darkness. The lilies were at his feet alongside the ruins of earlier donations. He was mumbling to himself in the silence of the night.

My Luger slipped into my hand. I stepped out from the bushes. I hit him with my prepared introduction. "Call me Lake. Water to your fire. And you are Vittorio Firenze."

He stiffened. His back straightened; his head came up. He didn't turn. He spoke out clearly. "That man is dead."

"Not yet." I circled round to where he could see me and got closer to him. His hooded eyes fixed their hawk gaze on my face, ignoring the gun.

"So Mister Lancelot, the knight, has come to kill the king? The dying king... My nemesis?"

Now he'd asked me, and it made me ask myself. Was I really going to slaughter him? Cold blood? I'd planned to get him alone, away from the Mansion and his guards. Maria, Donna, my mother—all their lives were at risk from this man. Lyra had asked me to take him out. I couldn't trust the Feds or the cops. It was all down to me. An anonymous hit in the dark. No mob revenge. No corrupt officials coming down on me. I just had to pull that trigger and vanish back to LA.

And here was the perfect place to end it. Poetic justice? I didn't know.

As the thoughts tumbled, convincing me, the new picture showed itself again. To stall, I blurted out, "Nemesis was a woman."

Maybe he spotted my uncertainty. "So..." He asked the same question he'd asked me at the Mansion. "What are you going to do?"

29. NEMESIS

I had him right there in front of me. Two slugs to the head, so it looked like a professional hit, and it was all over.

Something held me back. I'd killed men in the war. But that was in hot combat. This was different. This was murder, however justified.

I stalled, played for time while I tried to convince my finger to squeeze. I ran through the new picture for my benefit, not his.

"Verity was your girl, your property, the hold you had over Sheriff Jackson and his contacts in the city.

"But she took up with your daughter. Bad mistake. You found out. Maybe caught them in bed together? Your special girl in bed with your own daughter. You didn't like that. Made you angry. Maybe crazy. Isn't there something about fathers and daughters? Which one were you most jealous of? So you punished Verity hard, too hard. Punished her till you killed her, right here in the basement. Maybe you intended to kill her?

"But you got scared. Jackson might act like a father at last and get on your tail, maybe prodding the Bureau to act. The syndicate wouldn't like that.

"Perhaps it was shame, or guilt, or fear…I don't know. You torched the cabin, faked your death, changed your name, your appearance. Cleared it with the Reno boys and came back as Caldera. They gave you the Mansion to keep you out of the way. You hid from your daughter. At first, she thought you were really dead, then she worked it out. She tried to meet with you, but you kept hiding. Guilt? Or just a new way of causing pain?

"You watched her through your one-way glass when she came to the Mansion.

"Marty knew, and a few others. You paid them off, but you were never sure. Started bumping them off. The surgeon was first, I guess. Did the servants really go back to Mexico? And later, Harry—"

"I know *nothing* of this Harry person but what I was told." His voice was slow but firm. Of all the deaths, he wanted to be absolved of that one. Just the one.

I took it on board for later and kept going. "But you keep coming back here to beg forgiveness. Verity was special."

All the while he was throwing glances over my shoulder, showing no fear. He looked confident, smug. "Yes. She was very special." Slowly, he raised his hands, spreading his arms wide like a man on a cross. He offered himself up as a target.

I'd seen men die in many ways, but never like this. Surrendering himself. Offering himself as a victim, as a holy sacrifice.

"If you're looking down the path and stalling, hoping for your driver to show, he won't be coming any time soon." Hell, I enjoyed saying that.

He covered his flicker of a reaction with a calm, cold tone. "When you've already died once, it holds no terror."

"But you didn't really die last time. This time's for real."

"Good point. But you aren't going to pull that trigger. You just don't have the *cojones*. You're no killer. Not a murderer. You don't have it in you or I'd be dead already." His mocking voice burned into my brain. But I still didn't pull the trigger.

The familiar hint of expensive perfume I had gotten to know well came to me. Verity? Here? Encouraging me?

Images hit me.

The crucifix on Harry's wall.

The silver crucifix around Isabella's throat as she lay dead on Maria's bed.

The torture furniture in the Mansion's dungeon.

The altar at Harry's funeral.

"Oh, I mean it, believe me. I really do mean it. For Verity." I slashed at his face with the pistol's barrel.

He yelled as he swayed to his right.

"For Isabella." Another swipe.

He fell to his knees in the mud and weeds in the ruins of his home. How many other hidden graves were there in the grounds? That's why he never sold the land. Too many secrets under the surface. The biggest secret of them all was his undying attachment to Verity.

Caldera changed as realization hit him harder than my barrel. His arrogance fell away. Wide-eyed, he shook with fear. He begged me to stop, to forgive him, to let him go.

From far away, I heard a car engine straining and roaring as it fought the slope and forest bends. It was getting closer. Time was running out. Maybe it was the local Mob. Maybe it was the cops. Maybe it was the Feds.

It was now or never. I pressed the pistol's muzzle against his forehead. His face bled from the pistol-whipping. He whimpered, a man broken. It was pathetic. The monster's humanity revealed. He was mumbling as he slipped into a personal hell. His bluster was gone. He knew what was coming. Finally, he believed me.

And he called on God, for Chrissakes. "Father, into your hands I commit my spirit…" His voice broke up in sobbing.

His insanity had risen. It shone in his eyes. It dribbled from his lips. It trembled in his fingers.

Still I hesitated, gun barrel against his temple. My hand trembled, but at this range I couldn't miss.

Underneath the arguments in my head, I heard his voice mumbling. A prayer for the acceptance of death. I let him finish.

"Most Sacred Heart of Jesus, I accept from Your hands whatever kind of death…"

But he was right. I was not a murderer.

The car engine had stopped.

"…it may please You to send me this night with all its pains, penalties and sorrows…"

The smell of the perfume grew stronger.

Through the pleadings, I heard footsteps on the gravel behind me.

I heard a voice. Lyra, commanding. "Kill him."

"…in reparation for all of my sins, for the souls in Purgatory…"

A pleading Spanish-accented female voice. Isabella. "Kill him."

"…for all those who will die today and for Your greater glory…"

And another, and another. A chorus of voices. "Kill. Kill. Kill."

Pounding in my ears.

"Amen."

Under them all, a different voice. A quiet voice rising, struggling to be heard. Donna's voice. "This is not you. Think. You are no murderer. You are a good man. Think!"

And my mom's voice, just the once. "You're a good man, son." She sounded weary, as if this world had become too much for her.

A good man? Was I a good man? What was it to be good in this filthy world?

The voices still battled in my head, many calling for me to kill, one lone voice begging me not to, and the last one, Mom, saying I was a good man.

A safety catch snicked off right behind me.

I had no more time to think.

I fired.

Someone behind me fired.

I tensed, expecting a bullet's pain to rip through me. Nothing. Caldera jerked once, fell back, and lay still in the mud.

I turned. In the moonlight, a woman, gun in hand, white-faced, an insane look in her eyes.

"Verity?" I raised my pistol, but she threw hers away into the weeds.

I knew I'd fired past him, hadn't killed him. Couldn't bring myself to do it. Verity had killed him. Verity. But Verity was dead. Was I insane?

No. It wasn't Verity. "Lyra?"

The dead man's daughter staggered past me, fell to her knees, bent low over his body, and buried her face in her hands.

I watched her, fascinated and revolted as the sobbing wracked her body. I dropped my ass onto a log, a surviving piece of the charred cabin. It'd been a long day. A long month. I was weary, confused, drained.

But I was not a murderer. Donna was right.

And nemesis was female. Right again.

Oh, how I wanted Donna's arms right then. I wasn't a murderer. But there was a whole mess to sort out, and it looked like I was the one who had to do it. Okay. But first I needed a smoke. My God, how I needed a smoke right then.

At my feet was a woman sobbing over a corpse: the man she'd just murdered.

Her own father.

Yeah, I needed a smoke.

30. MIST ON THE WATER

I'd seen death. Many times. Too many times. I remembered the deaths in the past weeks and other deaths in other lands. But this was new.

She needed a while to work through what she'd done, the pain, the guilt, all that crap. But I itched for that smoke, and I decided she'd had enough time. I draped my jacket over her shoulders and lifted her to her feet. I turned her around and held her close for a while, letting her tears soak into my shoulder.

I'd never seen her so genuinely vulnerable. Neither of us spoke for the longest time. When she calmed, I guided her out of the ruins and down to the jetty. I offered her a Lucky. She smiled as she took it, her cheeks wet, her mascara smeared. We sat on the boards in silence and smoked until dawn lightened the surface of the lake and the surrounding forest.

She said just one thing, like it explained it all. "Verity loved it here, the mist on the water." Then she broke up in sobbing again.

I needed to know more. "You followed me here?"

Her head shook. "You told me this day was marked in his diary. That night when we… I worked out what it meant."

So I had killed him, in a way. But I didn't pull the trigger.

Some consolation. It was messy.

Life was messy. It didn't come all nicely wrapped up like a Christmas gift.

Lyra had her problems. I had mine.

I still wasn't sure who'd killed Harry or who really paid Mom's trust fund—which Firenze could I believe, father or daughter? Was Sheriff Jackson's involvement really only shame and greed? There was something really dirty in the Bureau. Nameless was still out there. Marty would be on the streets again soon… And where was Maria?

More important was Donna's secret. Maybe she'd tell me her story, when she was ready.

Like I said, life ain't a nicely wrapped Christmas gift.

But the ghost that had driven me was surely satisfied now. Exorcised? Was that the word? Had to ask Donna. Plenty of time to dig deeper. For now, I just wanted to get back to Donna for some more pampering. She was the only wholesome thing to come from this whole mess. Wholesome. Good word. A Donna word.

Except Donna had secrets, too. Even Donna.

I stood, flicking my last Lucky's butt spinning away into the water. "It's time."

She nodded. "I know. It's okay. I did what I had to. It's over now. Time to see the police. Time to tell."

Yeah. And time for me to get back to Donna. Maybe I'd hug her tight; maybe I wouldn't. Maybe I'd tell her how I felt; maybe I wouldn't.

Hell, the future'd sort itself out. Always did.

As we reached the tree line, I turned to grab one last look across the waters. A morning mist rose from the lake's surface. For a moment, I thought I caught the pale shape of a woman— blond hair, big smile, dressy white gown as if for some swanky party.

Or for the Mansion.

But as I looked, the image faded, and it was just a mist on the water.

The End

Next in the series will be "Public Lies"

ABOUT THE AUTHOR

If you've read this far, you probably thought the story wasn't too bad. Glad you enjoyed it.

Andy was abducted by science fiction pulp magazines in his early teens and fell in love with black-and-white noir movies soon after. After graduation he worked in marketing, franchising, and computing in London and Luxembourg before launching his own web design company. In 2011, he sold the company and retired early to write, act, and travel.

He hopes you enjoy reading the adventures of his imaginary friends.

Other Works:
Check out Andy's published novels and short stories:
andymckell.com/bibliography

Newsletter:
Sign up at **bit.ly/andynoirs** for updates, background info, price promotions, competitions, and even an occasional free story.

Authors Love Recommendations (and Reviews):
Explore Andy's other fiction, tell your friends, and any review you'd like to drop with the distributor of your choice would be really appreciated! *Thanks in advance!*

Blog: **andymckell.com**
Goodreads: **goodreads.com/AndyMcKell**
Facebook: **facebook.com/AndyMcKell.Author**

Acting Credits:
bit.ly/AndyScreen
bit.ly/AndyStage

Lightning Source UK Ltd.
Milton Keynes UK
UKHW022024090223
416682UK00015B/2019